ENDURING
BREEZE

BY
ED ROBINSON

(I always say that). The descriptions of what took place during and after Hurricane Irma are all too real for my wife and I, as Breeze and Brody relive the events that we experienced in real life.

For my mother, who always encouraged me to succeed in my chosen endeavors.

"When best-laid plans have fallen to waste
And frustration abounds in their former place
When failure looms with doubts and fears
We must endeavor to persevere."
Endeavor to Persevere, George Wooten

"We thought about it for a long time, *Endeavor to Persevere.*" When we had thought about it long enough, we declared war on the Union."
Lone Watie in The Outlaw Josie Wales

If, therefore, we wish that Christ should reckon us to be his disciples, we must endeavor to persevere.
John 8:31

One

A major hurricane was headed right for us. Her name was Irma, and she was a bitch. We'd returned to Palm Island Marina after seeing off Holly and Daniel. We were living the good life complete with electricity, unlimited water, and a pool. All had been well until Irma threatened to destroy us.

She'd already devastated the Middle Keys and was churning across Florida Bay, regaining what little strength she'd lost after her brief encounter with those islands. Both the local news and the Weather Channel had issued dire warnings. Irma was a formidable storm with life-threatening potential. Our area was expected to see winds over one-hundred and thirty miles per hour. The storm surge could be ten to fifteen feet.

In all my years living aboard a boat in Florida, I'd never had to deal with a direct hit from a hurricane of any size. This one was a Category Five and seemed determined to teach me a lesson. If I had been alone, I'd have taken *Leap of Faith* to a good hurricane hole and ridden it out. Brody wanted nothing to do with that plan. The marina wouldn't allow us to remain in the slip. They offered to haul us out and store the boat inside their dry storage building. They wanted two thousand dollars for this service. I thought that if the predicted conditions came true, that building would be gone. I decided to anchor her close enough to the marina that I could come back to shore in the dinghy. I hated to leave her to her own devices, but it was the best plan that Brody and I could agree on. She rented us a condo to stay in during the storm.

We worked for days stripping the boat down. All the canvas was removed. Biminis were taken down. The solar panels were stored in the condo. I'd recently purchased new heavy-duty chain and a storm anchor. Brody removed our valuables and took them to the condo as well. I didn't own much and didn't give it much thought. I was, however, very worried about *Miss Leap*. I puzzled over anchoring for the coming doomsday. I had three anchors and decided to use them all. I chained them together in a thirty-foot triangle formation, using the biggest as the centerpiece. I rigged up a new chain bridle and decided to wrap the last of the chain around my Sampson post. If the bridle broke, the windlass wouldn't hold in high winds. I made a checklist of all the things that needed to be done before we abandoned the boat. Neither one of us could stop watching the weather.

For several days the weather-guessers had assured us that Irma would be an East Coast event. That was changing by the hour. After each update, the storm track inched further and further west. At the last minute, our local weather guy drew a bullseye around our marina. His advice was to evacuate.

The marina staff was scrambling to haul all the boats that wanted to be hauled. The dock master asked me what I was going to do. I told him we were leaving soon. Brody was in a panic. Our neighbor Bruce was on a sailboat that wouldn't fit inside the building. He didn't have the cash to pay for hauling out anyway. Brody offered for him to stay with us in the condo. We tied his boat up as best we could and turned our attention back to *Leap of Faith*. Bruce agreed to help me deploy my anchoring rig. I fired up the engine. Brody and Bruce untied us from the dock. I put the transmission in reverse to back out of the slip. Nothing happened. We just sat there.

"What the hell?" I said.

"She doesn't want to leave," said Brody.

"Tie her back up," I yelled.

Bruce shrugged. The dock master shrugged.

"I can't leave if she won't move," I told him. "Give me a bit. Let me see what's going on."

I went below to the engine room. There was no fluid on the dipstick for the transmission. Where'd it go? I sent Brody to the hardware store for more transmission fluid. I poured in what I had and flushed it back out. It wasn't pretty. When Brody returned I repeated the process until the fluid looked clean. The transmission went into gear. The lines were untied a second time and we made our way out of the marina. There was one other boat that had decided to anchor for the storm. Captain Lee took his big old Hatteras into Rum Bay. I took *Miss Leap* down to Don Pedro Island. There was a little piece of water just off the ICW called Kettle Cove. No other boats were there. Bruce and I threw the two lead anchors off either side of the bow. I played out chain until the big storm anchor dropped off the bow pulpit. We drifted slowly back until almost all the chain was in the water. I rigged the bridle and wrapped the chain around the Sampson Post. It scratched the hell out of the finish, but I couldn't worry about that.

We'd dropped the anchors in eight feet of water. By the time we'd settled down, we were sitting in six feet of water. With two hundred feet of chain out, the boat could rise up on the surge without dislodging the anchors. At least that's what I hoped. I closed the seacock and turned off all the electrical systems. I plugged up the exhaust hole with a foam stopper. I took a last look around before telling the others to get in the dinghy. As we started to head back to the marina, I couldn't help looking back. *Miss Leap* looked sad all stripped bare. I was leaving her. I could only hope that I would see her again. Life had gotten pretty good for me over the past year or two. I had more money than I could spend. I had Brody. Things couldn't be more perfect. That would change drastically if I lost *Leap of Faith*. Brody had come to love the old boat too.

"Is she going to make it?" she asked.

"I don't know," I admitted. "I figure those anchors will hold her in most anything. We've done all we can."

We went back to the condo and turned on the news. It wasn't good. We were under a mandatory evacuation. The storm was now predicted to ride right up the west coast of Florida, putting us on the worst side of it. It would run just barely offshore, pounding the coastal areas with extreme wind and waves. The local weatherman was pulling no punches.

"Get out," he said. "If you stay, you'll die."

His storm surge map showed our marina under at least ten feet of water. The Gulf of Mexico would overtake our condo, the marina buildings, and everything in its path. The barrier islands had already been evacuated. They would be destroyed.

"What are we going to do?" asked Brody.

"Let's give it until morning," I said. "If the forecast holds, we'll bug out."

"To where?" she said. "We have no place to go."

"We'll drive north until we're safe," I told her. "Get a room somewhere."

"What about our stuff?" she asked. "We can't take all of it."

"Put it up high," I said. "Take only what we need. Get food and water. We'll only be gone a few days."

We packed our little car with essentials and gassed it up. I had twelve gallons of extra gas that I put in the trunk. The traffic out of Florida was a big issue. The news showed huge backups and multiple wrecks on I-75. Many gas stations were out of fuel. We debated over staying or leaving. In the end, I had to defer to Brody. She wanted to evacuate, so that's what we did. Bruce decided to stay behind. We wished him well. Captain Lee was originally going to stay aboard his boat. As the forecast worsened, he changed his mind. He tried to come ashore but his dinghy outboard wouldn't run. His wife called and begged me to go get him. I assured her that I would, as soon as I finished with my own preparations. By the time I called him, he'd secured another ride. I liked him. I hoped that his boat survived. He took his family over to the other coast. We wished each other well and went about the business of escaping.

The forecast was no better in the morning. The forecast track was still awful. According to the talking heads on the television, anyone remaining in the evacuation areas was doomed. Irma was about to end life as we knew it on the west coast of Florida.

"Let's roll," I told Brody.

"Are we going to be all right?" she asked.

"We'll be better away from here," I said. "Let's go right now."

We said goodbye to Bruce and his little dog Scupper and drove away from the marina. It was a weird feeling leaving everything behind. The streets were deserted until we picked up I-75. The late leavers like us had packed the highway bumper to bumper. We crawled north as far as Bradenton. I took us off the freeway and onto old route 301. The pace was a little better. When we saw an open station we stopped for gas. The further north we went, the fewer open stations we saw. We saw fellow refugees with gas cans strapped to the roof and cars packed to the gills with belongings. Everyone was anxious. There were fender benders and frayed nerves at every little town. We stayed on 301 almost all the way to Georgia. We picked up I-95 and the traffic slowed again. We had not made good time. It was getting dark as we took the off ramp for Kingsland, Georgia. We sat in a parking lot and called a bunch of hotels. We could see them all over the place, but no one was answering the phone. Finally, a clerk told us that they too were under a mandatory evacuation. The hotels were all closed. We were tired and frazzled with no place to sleep.

Brody called the national number for Holiday Inn. The woman told her that the closest available room she had was in Charleston, South Carolina. We booked it. It was still a long way up the road, but we didn't want to sleep in the car. The seats didn't recline, and we'd packed too much stuff to be able to lie down. I drove on through the night. It was late when we made our way into town. Brody's phone didn't give us the greatest directions. We missed our turn. We ended up in the ghetto section of Charleston. We circled back and again missed the turn. We got it right on the third try, but only after driving down Crack Street. I was completely out of my element. I was frustrated. Brody was cranky too, but happy to have finally made it. We carried some bags into our room and turned on the TV.

Jim Cantore was in Naples. Some other goober from the Weather Channel was in Punta Gorda, wearing a flak jacket and helmet. A third idiot stood in a mud puddle in Miami, pretending that the wind was about to blow him over. A couple on bicycles rode by in the background. The big red radar blob that was Irma continued to churn towards our home. I kicked off my shoes and dug out a bottle of rum. I was still vibrating from the road. We watched the weathermen until we fell asleep.

The first thing we did in the morning was turn on the TV. Hurricane Irma had maintained her track through the night. All of the models were in agreement. Our little slice of paradise was in deep trouble, especially *Miss Leap*.

"It's time to consider the possibility that we won't have a boat to go home to," I said.

"I can't even think about it," said Brody. "She's got to make it. Have faith in her, Breeze."

"We put her in an impossible situation," I said. "That damn storm is going to cover the whole state of Florida. There was nowhere to run to."

"We did the best we could for her," she said. "It's out of our hands now."

We found a grocery store and stocked up on food. I got a six-pack too. We spent the day pacing the halls and watching the storm. We saw it take a jog inland towards Marco Island. We saw flooding in Miami. The state of the Keys was largely still unknown. There was no power or cell phone communication there. Marco got it bad. I started to gain some hope as we watched the storm track slightly more inland. Then we saw pictures of Charlotte Harbor and the ICW where we'd left *Leap*. All the water was gone. It had been sucked out to sea. That meant that our boat was lying on her side, sitting in the mud instead of floating. I'd prepared for a big surge, but I hadn't thought of this. I didn't like it. She was an old boat, and not designed to lay over like that. I started envisioning all the problems that might occur. She was probably dumping fuel out the vent. Her contents were all strewn to one side. What little water that was left could enter the cabin in any number of places, especially when it started to come back in. On the plus side, she wasn't going to drag anchor. Her fate depended on the timing of the storm and the tide's return.

We couldn't stop watching the news. I used Brody's phone to keep an eye on the weather radar throughout the day. I watched intently as it tracked to the east of Palm Island Marina. That put us on the less severe side. *Leap of Faith* had a fighting chance. Naples saw winds to ninety miles per hour. Punta Gorda airport reported gusts over ninety, but no sustained winds over eighty. The Cape Haze Peninsula had somehow dodged the worst of it. The coastal areas up to Tampa Bay were mostly spared as well. The storm ripped and gouged its way up the center of the state and into Georgia. Now it was headed towards us in Charleston. What the hell? We'd driven five hundred miles to escape and now what was left of the hurricane was bearing down on us once again.

The power went out just before dark. Tornados spun up along the Carolina coast. Flood waters breached the sea wall and inched up the street towards the hotel. I went outside to move our car up into a parking garage. Others weren't so fortunate. Half a dozen cars were flooded to the dashboards in the parking lot. Construction cranes next door spun wildly in the wind. The swimming pool was inundated with flood waters as well. Our room was on the first floor. The water was lapping at the sliding glass doors.

Darkness fell. I tried to go outside to get a look at things, but the hotel manager stopped me.

"We've got a tornado nearby," he said. "Please stay in your room."

"Where we've got no air conditioning and no television," I said. "Don't you have a generator for this place?"

"We're working on it, sir," he said. "Please be patient."

I was not patient. I wanted out of that place. The water was too deep to leave though, and the bridge out of town had been closed. We were trapped. Brody produced a battery powered light out of her luggage. We sat and ate sandwiches in the soft glow of LEDs.

"This is messed up," she said.

"We'll get out of here in the morning," I told her. "As soon as the water recedes."

She used her phone to keep up on the news. The morning would bring a low tide and an opportunity to leave Charleston. Authorities were urging everyone to stay off the roads to allow emergency crews to work. Flooding was rampant from Miami to Jacksonville. The interchange at I-10 and I-75 was closed due to flooding. Thousands of trees were down and very few places had power. I didn't care. We were leaving at the first opportunity. We still had twelve gallons of gas in the trunk. We had some water and snacks. We had to get back to *Miss Leap*.

Two

Brody's phone was just about dead and we had no way to recharge it. The hotel was full of other refugees in the same boat. Folks complained and begged for the manager to do something. They were worried about their homes and family members who didn't evacuate. The manager enlisted some help and stole a big wheeled generator from the construction site next door. Four men pushed and pulled it through waist-deep water and parked it in front of the hotel entrance. Extension cords were produced. Pandemonium ensued as dozens of people tried to charge their phones at the same time. Brody fought the mob while I drank rum in the dark of the room. She was gone a long time.

I went to look for her and was taken aback by the scene. Bad news was pouring in from all across Florida. I watched a man who'd just learned that the roof was gone from his home. He sank to the floor and put his head in his hands, wondering if there would be anything left to salvage. He'd just returned from Texas, where he'd helped his son recover from hurricane Harvey. A woman with a baby was going around begging for wet wipes. Brody appeared and told her that she had some in the room. They walked down the hall in the darkness. The baby cried.

I elbowed my way through the scene at the generator to assess the water levels. They were coming down. The tornado warning had been lifted. I got our bags from the room and waded through thigh-deep water to the parking garage. We'd be ready to go in the morning. Brody contacted a friend who had access to NASA satellites. Some had been repurposed to zoom in on the hurricane damage. She explained where we'd left the boat, eventually sending him an image from Google Maps. It didn't take him long. He sent back a fuzzy picture of a boat floating in Kettle Cove, just behind Don Pedro Island. We'd been the only boat there when we left. It had to be ours. I studied the picture hard, looking for obvious signs that it was indeed *Miss Leap*. I simply couldn't be sure, but the odds were in our favor. It had to be her.

Then Brody got a text from a friend in the marina. They'd trespassed through an exclusive estate property to try to get a look at our boat. They took a picture from the shoreline. There, a few hundred yards away, was *Leap of Faith*. She was floating, right where we'd left her. She was listing a bit to port, but there she was. She'd survived. Brody let out a whoop. We hugged and smiled like we'd just won the lottery.

Long live *Leap of Faith*.

If you've never loved a boat like I have, you won't understand. People see boats as inanimate objects. They see them as replaceable things. That was not true for me. I saw her as a living, breathing entity. She'd been my best friend through it all. Sometimes, she'd been my reason for living. If she hadn't made it through the storm, I would have suffered an incalculable loss. I was still worried about her, though. That list meant something was wrong. We had to get back to her as soon as possible.

The water had receded enough by morning for us to leave. There was no power still in Charleston, but we found an open gas station a few miles up the road. It took over an hour to get back out to I-95 and head south. Traffic was heavy but moving. In spite of the warnings from authorities, the road was full of returning refugees. Power trucks and lineman fought with the cars for space. The exits in Georgia were blocked by National Guardsmen. People were being told it wasn't safe to return home. Trees were down everywhere. Folks were on the side of the road, out of gas.

We took the beltway around Jacksonville to I-10 West to avoid a pileup. We picked up 301 South and encountered a mess. There were no traffic lights. No one had power. Each intersection was a dangerous gamble. There was no gasoline to be had. We stopped north of Ocala and poured our reserve gas into the car's tank. It was just enough to fill us up, but not enough to get us home. We decided to try I-75 to avoid the dangerous intersections with no stoplights. It was heavily packed and moving at a snail's pace. I couldn't stand it. I jumped off onto the Florida Turnpike that ran to Orlando. The first exit was for 301. I took it. We dealt with the lack of traffic signals for a few more hours. Brody needed to pee. We couldn't find an open place for her to go. Finally, she went behind a closed gas station. I went back there after she was done. Another man took my place when I left.

We stretched a bit and considered our options. 301 was a nerve-wracking mess. 75 was crawling. Then we heard on the radio that the traffic jam had cleared south of the turnpike exit. We decided to try our luck on 75 again, except the GPS on Brody's phone got me lost. We ended up in Tampa. I cursed modern technology. If we'd only had a damn map. I pulled off in a parking lot and Brody got our bearings. We made a U-turn and took some cross-town expressway back to 75. We found it moving, but with heavy traffic. My nerves were raw at this point. Brody tried to calm me.

"We're almost there," she said. "Just a little further."

We took the River Road exit towards Englewood. I was grateful to be off the freeway. The damage here was less severe than in Central Florida. When we arrived at the marina, not much was out of place. A portion of the seawall had collapsed and some trees were down, but that was about it. We found Bruce watching TV in the condo. He said he never lost power. He was enjoying the air conditioning while we sweated in the dark in South Carolina. His boat was fine. I suggested that he return to it and leave me and Brody alone. He collected his little dog and left.

Our dinghy had been stored inside a marina building, which had weathered the storm well. It was too late to go out to the boat, though. We were both exhausted from the thirteen-hour drive. As much as I wanted to go out to her, *Miss Leap* was going to have to wait until the next morning. After a few shots of rum, I hit the sack and slept like a rock.

When we woke, we were both anxious to go see *Leap.* I rounded up our dinghy, gassed it up, and picked up Brody from the condo. It was just over a mile ride until we could see her. She was indeed leaning sharply to port. The chain bridle was intact. One side window cover was missing. I tied off to her and we climbed aboard. A quick check of the bilge showed some water, but not enough to make her lean so badly. What was there couldn't make it to the bilge pump in order to be pumped out. I grabbed a shop vac and sucked up the water. There was no change in how the boat was listing. I checked in the lazarette. There was no water there. I couldn't figure out why she was leaning. I emptied the port side water tank. It made no difference. I sat and thought it over. Brody was inspecting the interior and finding evidence of water intrusion here and there.

A potential cause dawned on me. I checked the starboard side fuel tank. It was empty. I checked the port side tank. It was full. I had one hundred and fifty gallons of diesel on one side, and zero gallons on the other. At roughly seven pounds per gallon, I had just over a thousand more pounds of weight on the port side, than on the starboard side. That would do it. Brody opened up the hatches to air her out. I attempted to bring in the anchors. I got the chain mostly in, but the lead anchor wouldn't budge. It was buried in deep. I needed some strong help.

After a quick chat with *Miss Leap*, when I assured her it was going to be okay, we went back to the marina to look for someone to help. Captain Lee had returned with his Hatteras. *Evergreen* didn't have a scratch on her. His two sons had come to help retrieve his boat. They were more than willing to give me a hand. Back we went to the anchorage. I opened the seacock and unplugged the exhaust. The engine fired up immediately. Lee's sons worked together to raise all three of my anchors. I nudged the boat into gear to break the first one free. The other two came up with less difficulty. That was all the transmission had for me. I tried to turn back towards the marina but had no propulsion. I had half a quart of transmission fluid left. I poured it in. The shaft started to turn very slowly. We crawled along at perhaps one knot. I didn't have enough speed to maintain steerage. There was no wind and little current, so we simply floated in place once the transmission stopped turning altogether.

Lee's boys jumped into action. They brought the dinghy around to the bow and tied off for a tow. The little outboard had a hard time, but we made progress towards the marina. The difficulty was still in steering. The big boat was too heavy to control with the tiny outboard. I called ahead to the marina, asking for assistance. I hated to do it, but I just wanted to put her safely in a slip so I could tend to her problems. Just as we approached the channel entrance, one of the mechanics came out in his flats boat. He was able to take us the rest of the way in, and get us close enough to the slip so that we could throw lines. Friends on the dock pulled us in the rest of the way. With a lot of help, I got *Leap of Faith* back home. I wasn't used to receiving so much kindness, but I was grateful.

Brody got to work cleaning and I got down in the bilge. There was oil and transmission fluid mixed with water everywhere. What a mess. I spent several days cleaning that up. I also worked the boatyards looking for advice on the transmission. I ended up calling a company out of Tampa. Their response was quick. The resolution was not. The old Paragon transmission was obsolete, and parts were difficult to find. At first, they told me it simply couldn't be rebuilt. My other option was to buy a new transmission from a different manufacturer. The engine would have to be realigned to make it work. I measured and took pictures for them. I didn't like the thought of moving the engine. It needed to go down a few inches, and there wasn't much room for that. The stringers that the mounts sat on were solid wood, twelve inches thick. Cutting into them would make me cringe.

Time passed with no progress on the transmission. I slowly put the boat back together. The bimini tops went back up, as did the solar panels. I'd discovered water in the oil. I assumed it came in through the breather and the dipstick. I hooked up my oil change bucket, but it wouldn't suck the oil out. The impeller was bad. I knew from experience that I'd never find one on a store shelf. Brody went online and ordered two, so we'd have a spare. Things continued like that. Every project was more difficult than it should have been.

I spent two days carrying diesel fuel in jugs from the fuel dock to the slip. Working in the Florida heat took its toll on me. Just as I'd straightened out the listing problem, I thought I'd pass out.

"Your face is red," said Brody. "You feeling okay?"

"No," I answered. "No, I am not."

She took me inside and gave me cool water. She made me lie down. I felt a heaviness in my chest. I didn't want to tell her, but she knew something was wrong.

"I'm going to find you a doctor," she said.

"I'm not going to the hospital," I replied. "I'll be fine in a little bit."

"Let me ask around," she said. "You just take it easy."

Captain Lee gave her the number of a clinic in Englewood. Brody called them and they said I could come right in. She drove me there. The first thing the doctor did was check my blood pressure. It was through the roof.

"It's dangerously high," he said. "I'm going to take some blood and run some tests. Limit your physical activity for a few days. I'm writing you a prescription."

I took the pills, limited my activity, and laid off the rum for a few weeks. My cholesterol was high, but my blood pressure came down. The doctor told me to eat less cheese, meat and sour cream. I said that sounded like the tacos I had for dinner. He said to cut down on the bacon and eggs. I said that's what I had for breakfast. I didn't like where this was going. I'd never had any sort of illness. I hadn't seen a doctor in decades. Suddenly, at fifty-five, I needed medicine. I was reasonably fit. I tried to keep myself in shape. I did drink too much from time to time. Doctor visits and prescription refills would seriously put a cramp in my style.

Meanwhile, we'd discovered that our rudder was out of its socket. There was a post on the bottom that fit into a bushing on the skeg. It had popped out and refused to go back in. A friend dove under to try to fix it but had no luck. A professional diver tried too. He couldn't fix it either, but wanted to try again once the transmission was fixed. The shaft had been pushed back, in order to remove the old transmission, and the prop was up against the rudder support. He sounded confident that he could get the job done.

The transmission guys eventually located all the parts to do a rebuild. They gave me a quote for that, and another quote for a new transmission and engine realignment. They were in the same ballpark. I went with the rebuild. It took them a few more weeks to get it done. Finally, installation day arrived. The guys worked hard and got everything put back together. They wanted to take a test drive, but I was worried about the rudder. We spun the transmission right there in the slip. It worked in both forward and reverse. I was satisfied with the work. I wasn't happy with the bill. At least I had the money to cover it. They were surprised when I paid them in cash.

I got the diver back and he was able to fix the rudder. Finally, we were making progress. We didn't really have any place to be, but just knowing that we were stuck drove us both crazy. That's when the battery bank died. When we drove to buy new batteries, the car broke down. We sat in a parking lot in Port

Charlotte, utterly frustrated. Brody called a friend at the marina to come pick us up. I called a tow truck. Our progress was delayed yet again.

The car got fixed and we got our new batteries. The impellers for the oil change pump came in and I took care of that. Then I moved on to the injector pump. An oddity of the Lehman 120 is that this pump doesn't get lubricated by the engine oil. It has its own oil supply that needs to be changed. When I unscrewed the drain plug, little bits of metal came out with it. The threads inside the pump were stripped. If ever there was a challenge to my blood pressure, it was at that moment. I was lying down in the engine room, staring at trouble once again. Since the hurricane, one problem after another had arisen. Most of them weren't even related to the storm. I thought maybe *Miss Leap* was punishing me for leaving her to face the storm alone. She hadn't wanted to leave the dock in the first place.

There was no easy solution to this new problem. The pump was a five thousand dollar item and a replacement was no simple task. There wasn't enough room under it to get a drill in there. I needed to re-tap the threads, but I didn't want to remove the pump. I tried an assortment of rubber expansion plugs, but they didn't hold. I was staring at the injector pump one day, watching a bead of oil form around the rubber plug, when I noticed a drip from somewhere else. It was coolant. A little pool of it had formed at the base of the sensor for the temperature gauge. I gave up on the plug and went to work on the sensor. I was confident I'd fixed the problem. When I started the engine again, I still saw the drip. I could barely see it, but a second sensor was hidden on the other side of the engine. When it leaked, the coolant ran over to the first sensor and pooled in the well that it sat in. I couldn't get to it from where I was. I could feel my pressure rising.

The access hatch for the area I needed to get to was under the settee. The settee was firmly attached to the floor, blocking the hatch. I'd never had a reason to open it. I didn't even know that particular sensor existed until that day. I got out my drill and worked to pull all the screws. I removed all of the stuff that Brody had stored under there. I pulled the settee out of the way, opened the hatch, and fixed the leak. I put everything back together and let out a big sigh. I'd been working for hours and still hadn't fixed the injector pump. I gave up for that day.

Three

Brody and I sat at the end of the dock with several other boaters to enjoy the sunset. A popular pastime at these gatherings was to bitch about our boat problems. I felt entitled to share the difficulties I'd been experiencing. A fellow named Gordon offered to help. He had a reputation as a good mechanic, so I accepted. He came over the next day to see what he could do. I'd bought a whole set of taps and dies just to get the one tool I needed. There wasn't room for us both down in the engine room, so he ended up doing all the work. I observed, learned what I could, and handed him things. I was secretly relieved that he'd jumped in and took over. Everything I'd touched recently had turned to shit.

Gordon was careful and methodical. He tapped out the new threads for a bigger bolt liked he'd done it a hundred times. The new bolt fit snugly and tightened properly. We took precautions not to leave any metal shavings inside the pump. He'd disassembled the raw water pump in order to make room to work. Once that was reassembled, the job was done. I used gasket maker to seal up the front plate, and I wanted to let it set up overnight before running the engine. I gave him my newly purchased toolkit for his troubles. I hope to never need it again. If I do, I can always look him up.

The next day everything checked out. The engine ran. The water pump flowed, and no oil leaked from the injector pump. *Leap of Faith* had been restored. She was ready to travel. That's when Brody got a call from the FBI. It was the last thing either of us expected. She talked for ten minutes with a concerned look on her face.

"They want me in D.C.," she said. "I'm to meet with the new director as soon as possible."

"Who is that these days?" I asked. "McCabe?"

"No," she said. "It's a guy named Christopher Wray. Trump appointed him after firing Comey."

"Your former employer seems to have its hands full of political intrigue these days," I said.

"It always has," she said. "Today's political climate seems to have amplified things."

"What's the word on this Wray fellow?"

"Depends on who you ask," she said. "He isn't considered a partisan operator. Supposed to be independent."

"But?" I asked.

"Buddies with Chris Christie. Donates to Republicans," she said. "Pretty mainstream otherwise. Seems like a safe pick."

"Why does he want to see you?"

"The Bureau has been greatly scrutinized since this whole Comey thing," she began. "Mueller too. They've managed to piss off both ends of the political spectrum. Wray is supposed to bring integrity back and regain the trust of the politicos in Washington. I'm afraid I'm a loose end."

"How so?"

"I was never technically terminated," she said. "I never resigned. Officially, I'm on an open-ended hiatus. That's how we left it."

"But it was your understanding that you wouldn't try to go back?"

"A lot has changed since then," she said. "I'm not surprised. Wray is doing what he's supposed to do. He's leaving no stone unturned."

"Do you know things that would worry him?" I asked.

"Possibly," she said.

"How could that affect your arrangement?"

"They'll probably want a non-disclosure agreement," she said.

"After grilling you about what you know and don't know," I suggested. "Bright lights and rubber hoses and shit."

"They can't afford to do something like that," she said. "D.C. is a minefield for them right now."

"So you'll be safe?"

"I have no reason to believe otherwise."

"I don't like it," I said.

"Why?" she asked. "What's to worry about?"

"I don't trust any of them for starters," I said.

"No one does," she said. "What else?"

"I just got the boat back in shape," I said. "I went through a lot of stress in the process. So much so that now I'm taking pills every day. Life's been out of whack ever since that damn hurricane showed up on the radar. Now, this.

The last thing we need is to deal with a bunch of political hacks in Washington."

"It's my problem," she said. "You don't have to deal with anything."

"Your problems are my problems," I said. "If you must go, I'll go with you."

"I have to go," she said. "It's the United States Government calling. I can't ignore it."

"Looks like we're taking a road trip," I said. "When do we leave?"

"Tomorrow," she said. "Let's pack a bag."

The drive north was much easier than our earlier trip. We weren't running for our lives. We stopped halfway and got a room for the night. I booked us a suite with a hot tub. The clerk looked at my cash like it was kryptonite. After securing a cold six-pack, I filled the tub. It wasn't in the bathroom, it was out in the middle of the suite, surrounded by mirrors. Seeing myself naked in the mirrors was kind of creepy, but I got over it when Brody stripped down. We soaked in the hot water and sipped cold beers.

"Aren't you worried?" I asked Brody.

"I'll just go in and see what they want," she said. "Until then I don't have enough information to form an opinion."

"It's got a bad feel to it," I said. "I spent too much time hiding from the FBI. Now we're having a sit-down with the head honcho."

"You won't be in the room," she said. "I'll be meeting them alone."

"Fine by me," I said. "Drop me at the bar. Matter of fact, let's get a room a couple hours away from your meeting. I don't need to go anywhere near that place."

"Don't be so paranoid," she said.

"It's not paranoia if they're really out to get you," I said. "What if they frown upon your association with me?"

"I hadn't considered that," she admitted. "It's all coming at me too fast."

"That's how they get your guard down," I said. "Step back and think things through. What do they really want from you?"

"I suppose I know a few things," she said.

"For example?"

"Comey used to work for John Ashcroft," she began. "He was Deputy Attorney General. Ashcroft was being pressured by the White

House over a secret domestic surveillance program, while he was sick in the hospital. His wife called Comey to intervene with White House counsel, who was about to barge into the hospital room. Comey called Mueller, who was then FBI Director. It was the start of a battle between the Justice Department and the White House. Both Comey and Mueller threatened to resign. This got them a meeting with President George W. Bush. He listened to them, agreed to restructure the program, and the resignation threats went away."

"What's all that got to do with you?" I asked.

"The whole thing almost came to blows," she said. The White House guys brought the Secret Service. Comey and Mueller brought FBI agents. I was one of them, picked only because I was available on a moment's notice and had nothing else to do. It was pretty intense."

"Where does Wray come in?"

"I forget what position he had at the time," she said. "But he backed Comey and Mueller. He was going to resign right along with them. Not too many people know that."

"And now he's stepping into the position they both once held," I said.

"Comey would have never become director if it wasn't for that incident," she told me. "He testified about it a few years later and came off looking like a hero. Now, after all this time, Wray has gotten his reward for standing by Comey and Mueller against the White House."

"Doesn't Trump know all this?" I asked.

"Who knows what Trump thinks or how he makes decisions?" she said. "But the Deep State dictates to the executive and legislative branches. It's been that way since Hoover."

"So the FBI got their own guy, a loyalist, no matter what Trump wanted?"

"He's also shown loyalty to Republicans," she said. "He's played the game well."

"No one is above politics," I said.

"Not in Washington," she said. "Not even Trump."

"This is why I don't pay any attention to politics," I said. "It all stinks and the stink comes from both sides."

"These guys aren't even elected," she said. "It's much greater than who wins a Senate seat or who controls the House. They're basically unaccountable."

"They didn't get to the top by being dumbasses," I offered.

"They didn't get there by being boy scouts either," she countered.

"Whatever attracted you to that field?" I asked.

"Oh I don't know, maybe protecting the Constitution," she said. "Fighting against all enemies, both foreign and domestic."

"You were a patriot," I said.

"Aren't you?" she asked.

"In my own way, I suppose. I did get some personal satisfaction from helping vets. I admire those guys. It's just that the FBI has been my enemy. I've been on their radar. Now you school me on some of their inner workings. They don't seem like patriots to me."

"Their loyalty lies with the Bureau, first and foremost," she said. "Trust me."

"The Company," I said.

"That's right," she said. "The Company. Inside The Company lies smaller allegiances and loyalties. Comey was true to Mueller. Wray was loyal to them both. That's how it works."

I got us another beer and tried to grasp what I was hearing. It was starting to make sense to me.

"It's not that different from the corporate world," I told her.

"Hold that thought while I try to picture you as a corporate stooge," she said, laughing.

"I paid my dues," I said. "I was loyal to the company."

"What came of it?" she asked.

"I was loyal to the wrong person," I said. "He took care of me, in the form of opportunities. In turn, I worked to make him look good. I did whatever he needed to be done. He walked me up the ladder and compensated me well."

"Sounds typical," she said. "What went wrong?"

"When you get close to the top, those alliances become critical," I explained. "My guy hit a dead end. He wasn't the favored son. His career was going nowhere."

"And neither was yours," she said.

"That's right," I said. "Hitched my wagon to the wrong horse, but at the time, it was the only horse I had."

"Any regrets?"

"None," I said. "He was a good man. He wanted what was best for the company. He did a good job. He just didn't win the political game."

"Why are you telling me this now?"

"I'm just trying to understand where you fit in all of this," I said. "Where do your loyalties lie?"

"Is this a trick question?" she asked. "I feel like you're getting into something deeper."

I suddenly didn't want to go any deeper. It was my fault for steering the conversation the way I had. I trusted Brody. I knew she loved me as much as I loved her. She'd given up her life to be with me, after all. Now her old life was coming back for her. It was a life where I could never fit in.

"This new FBI Director is going to want to see that you are loyal to The Company," I said. "Isn't that what this is all about?"

"I suppose so," she said.

"Are you?"

My question hung in the humid air over the hot tub for too long. Brody got out and wrapped herself in a towel. She got us each another beer and sat on the side of the tub.

"I just don't know anymore, Breeze," she said. "I'm far removed from that world, thanks to you. I don't know what I'm walking in to."

"Never a good position to be in," I advised.

"What can I do?"

"Do you still have any contacts?" I asked. "Someone who might know what's going on?"

"I can try," she said.

"It's either that or run," I said. "We can go back to the boat right now and disappear forever."

"We can't run from the FBI," she said.

"I did," I said. "They never caught me."

"I found you," she said.

"But you don't work there anymore," I said. "You're on my team now."

"I can't run," she said. "Not yet. Not until I find out what's up. Let me make some calls."

Brody had been gone for too long. No one had any information for her. They acted surprised that she called. They claimed to know nothing about it. Either they were lying or the new director had kept the meeting secret.

"I'm a capable woman," Brody said. "I'm just going to walk in there and hear them out. We'll go from there."

"It's entirely up to you," I said. "Keep me out of it."

"I'm not driving for hours to get to HQ either," she declared. "There are plenty of hotels nearby. We'll go right downtown. You can find a way to entertain yourself."

"Hey, I told you," I said. "A bar is all I need."

"Plenty of those too."

We drove downtown the next day. Brody checked us into the Grand Hyatt, just a few blocks away from the FBI's headquarters. I spotted a rum bar on the way in. We were in a concrete jungle that I didn't much care for. Brody was going in blind, and I didn't care much for that either. I couldn't help her with this. She was on her own. I just hoped that when it was over, I wouldn't be on my own.

We didn't talk much about it that night. The issue was settled. We ate a nice dinner, made soft quiet love, and went to sleep.

"I love you, Brody."

"Love you too, Breeze."

Brody dressed in a sharp business suit. She looked nice, if not a little stern. I guess FBI agents aren't supposed to look sexy. She didn't show any outward signs of nervousness. She was all business. I was forced to wear long pants because it was chilly outside. I stuck with the flip flops though, as a matter of protest. I walked with her for two blocks until we came to the Cuba Libre Rum Bar. That was my stop. She turned right on Pennsylvania Avenue and walked on without looking back. I went inside and asked for a menu.

There were two big tables pushed together next to the bar. A bunch of guys sat laughing and drinking. All of them had at least one prosthetic leg. Several wore patches on their clothing depicting what branch of the service they'd served in. At the head of the table was a guy with both of his original legs. I eavesdropped on their conversations. They belonged to an organization that helped disabled vets. They were in town for an event tomorrow. It was some sort of hike at Rock Creek Park, which was nearby.

I ordered some lunch and a beer and listened to their war stories. When they finished up their lunch, I introduced myself to the head guy. His name was Troy Warshel. I asked if I could buy him a drink. We sat at the bar and I asked about his group.

"The project is called Enduring Warrior," he said, handing me his card. "It's founded by veterans. Our mission is to honor and empower our wounded vets through physical, mental and emotional rehabilitation."

"How can I help?" I asked.

"You can donate at the website," he said.

"I'll do that," I said. "But is there anything hands-on that I can do?"

"We're looking for trainer-athletes," he said. "No offense, but it might not be your cup of tea."

"I'm in shape," I said.

"Come to Rock Creek Park tomorrow at nine," he said. "Wear some hiking boots. You saw those guys that were sitting here? Every one of them will kick your ass."

"Even with one leg?"

"That's right," he said. "You still want to come?"

"I'll be there," I said. "As long as there's cold beer afterward."

"Sure man," he said. "See you in the morning."

I bought a pair of hiking boots on the way back to the hotel. I wouldn't use them more than once, but I wanted to see what this Enduring Warrior project was all about. Something about those guys in the rum bar inspired me. A little hike in the woods wouldn't hurt.

Brody came back around five. As well as I knew her, I could not decipher how she felt about her meeting. She looked ambivalent.

"Well?" I said.

"Full reinstatement effective immediately," she said. "Benefits active, a big jump in pay grade, and the assignment of my choice."

"Holy shit," I said.

"The closest field office to us is in Tampa," she said.

"Wait, wait, wait," I said. "What's behind this offer? How did this play out?"

"Bring me into the fold," she explained. "My loyalty will be assured."

"Did you discuss the issues that might be of interest to the new director?"

"We did," she said. "He was very pragmatic."

"So he can just buy you off with a job and a pay raise?"

"There's nothing to buy off," she said. "I have no interest in spilling any beans that would hurt the Bureau."

"So what if you say no?"

"I was not given that option," she said.

"Of course you have that option," I said. "Don't be ridiculous."

"I was given a direct order from one of the highest law enforcement officials in the land," she said. "I'm to return to duty. No ifs, ands or buts."

"You have no rights to ignore or disobey?"

"Obey now, grieve later," she said. "That's the way it is. They sweetened the pot so I'd have no grievance later."

"What about free will?" I asked. "This is still America."

"It's a great opportunity," she said, staring at the floor.

"An opportunity yes," I said. "But the absolute demand is beyond troublesome. What kind of threats did they make if you don't accept?"

"Nothing specific," she said. "It was just made clear that it would be against my best interests to say no."

"How much time do you have?"

"A week."

"Good," I said. "Because I'm going hiking tomorrow."

I showed her the boots I'd bought and told her about Enduring Warrior. It was a handy way to divert the conversation away from the FBI. It only worked for a few minutes.

"What am I going to do, Breeze?" she asked.

"It's not up to me," I said. "But if you're asking, I say we get on our old boat and disappear. Fuck the FBI. We'll send them a postcard from Australia."

"They asked about you," she said. "They know we're together."

"What's my reputation inside the glorified halls of the FBI?"

"Shady," she said. "Our continued association would be frowned upon."

"No kidding," I said. "Did you expect anything less?"

"Look, I didn't ask for this to happen," she said. "It's not my fault."

"Nothing is your fault until you decide," I said. "The choice is clear. You can have a respectable career as an agent, or you can be with me. Money isn't part of the equation. We've got plenty."

"Running from the very agency that is offering me an excellent opportunity is part of the equation," she said. "But so is losing you."

"I've got no problem with running," I said. "I've had lots of experience. Hell, if you take the job they'll probably come after me anyhow.

In case you told me something you shouldn't have."

"Do you really believe that?" she asked.

"You're the G-man," I said. "Would you put it past them?"

"I guess it's a possibility," she admitted.

"So I'll be running either way," I said. "With or without you."

"I'm so sorry, Breeze," she said. "Sorry to screw things up like this."

"There was a time when I would have been too proud to beg you to stay," I told her. "You've changed all that. I don't want you to leave. Come away with me. Together, we can stay gone. They'll never find us. We can't let what we have end."

"I know we can't," she said. "But we're talking about the FBI. Frankly, I'm afraid of what they might do if they find us."

"We'll just have to make sure that never happens," I said. "The heat will blow over eventually. We'll be forgotten."

"Let me sleep on it," she said. "Go do your hike thing tomorrow and then we'll decide, together."

Four

Brody tossed and turned most of the night. I couldn't sleep as a result. When she settled down I finally dozed off. This caused me to wake up late. I grabbed a cup of coffee and a cold bagel off the hotel breakfast bar and took off for the park.

The warriors were ready to leave when I arrived. There was no time for introductions, which was a shame. I wanted to talk to some of them. I laced up my new boots and got in line. Troy led us in cadence, Marine Corps style. The pace was brisk. These guys were serious. This was no nature walk. I was fine for the first few miles, but the new boots rubbed my feet wrong. Then we hit some hills that wore me down. Before I knew it, I was at the back of the pack. My pride forced me to keep up with the other guys, but I really wanted to stop and rest.

Gradually, I fell back even more. I was indeed getting my ass kicked by a bunch of guys with prosthetic legs. My chest grew tighter and I had trouble breathing. Their pace only increased. I dug down deep and tried to regain contact with the pack. I was gaining on the last guy, who had lost both of his legs. When I caught up with him, he asked how I was doing.

"You okay back here?" he asked.

"Did you drop back just to check on me?" I asked. "Don't do that. Go on ahead."

"Gives me a good excuse to slow down," he said. "I'm still trying to get used to these new legs. I think I've got blisters on my stumps."

"You guys are incredible," I told him. "I didn't realize."

"Shit," he said. "You should have seen me when I had my real legs. I'd break all these guys down with a fifty-pound pack on my back."

"Guess I'm not in as good a shape as I thought," I said.

"Just keep pushing," he said. "It's not much further. You can do it."

There I was, in some forest near Washington, getting encouragement from a man who'd lost both legs. I came here thinking I could help somehow, but he was helping me. It was a real eye-opener. I thought maybe I'd just hand Troy some cash on my way out. He didn't need me slowing his guys down. Then I thought of Daniel. He would be a perfect fit with this group. He was young and in great shape. He was a Marine, but I didn't know where he was. I missed him. I suppose I missed Holly too, but being with Brody solved that for me. Then I remembered why we were here in the first place and the choice that Brody faced. My feet hurt. My chest was pounding. I put it all away and concentrated on marching forward. My new buddy was at my side, urging me on. For some reason, it was of the utmost importance that I finish. I might have been last, but I didn't give up. I didn't want to let him down. I didn't want to let the whole group down.

Then I saw Troy at the finish line. He was holding up a beer and waving me in.

"Come on, man," he yelled. "It's nice and cold."

I kept it up until I crossed the line, grabbing that beer on my way by. I made my way to a picnic table before opening it. I drank half of it on the first gulp. I took off my boots and examined my feet. Both heels were blistered badly.

"Anybody want a pair of size tens?" I asked.

"I'll take the left one," somebody said.

The whole group laughed in unison.

"Anybody need a right foot size ten?"

I sat and talked with Troy for a long time afterward. He explained how and why he'd signed on with Enduring Warrior.

"I'm a retired Marine Corps fighter pilot," he said. "I flew F/A-18s. I did several tours as a Forward Air Controller including a tour with Task Force Tawara in Iraq. We saw combat in An Nasiriyah. We were in the heaviest fighting early in Iraq up until the Battle of Fallujah. I had the opportunity to participate in the rescue of Jessica Lynch and the other members of her convoy."

"That's some impressive action," I said.

"Then my oldest son became a Marine Machine Gunner," he continued. "He did two deployments in Afghanistan where he lost a lot of friends to IEDs. After I retired, I decided I needed to do something about the IED problem. I went to work for the Army Counter IED Division where I managed a budget of 1.8

billion dollars developing solutions to detect and protect against IEDs."

"Did you come up with solutions?" I asked.

"As it turns out, a goat herder with a better idea can often defeat a multi-million dollar solution," he said.

"That's too bad," I said. "But it's what I expected you to say. Where'd you go from there?"

"I found a position with the Office of the Secretary of Defense for Operational Energy," he told me. "Our mission is to provide energy solutions that cut down on the use of fuel used on the battlefield. That translates into fewer fuel convoys and less risk for our troops."

"Does it make for a more effective fighting force?" I asked.

"Absolutely," he responded. "It sounds like you served."

"I did a stint in the Army," I said.

"What made you choose the Army?"

"I was young and dumb and just not going anywhere," I started. "I was still close to my father, who was an Army lifer. I told him I just didn't know what to do with my life. He told me to join the Army. Do my time, and if I didn't like it, move on to something else. I took his advice for lack of a better alternative. Dad took me to a recruiter buddy of his. He took me to take the ASVAB. I could take any job I wanted."

"What was your MOS?" he asked.

"Behavioral Science," I answered. "I was into psychology at the time, or thought I was."

"What kind of job did that translate into?

"They put me into drug and alcohol counseling," I said. "But first I had to go through Basic Medical. The recruiter didn't tell me that."

"You were a medic?"

"If you want to call it that," I said. "Ten weeks on a hospital campus at Fort Sam. I was in no way prepared to be a combat medic."

"How'd the drug and alcohol counseling gig go?"

"I wasn't qualified for that either," I told him. "Hell, not drinking was frowned upon. What I did was explain to guys how not to get into trouble when they were drinking, and how to handle an Article Fifteen when they did get in trouble. I guided them through the Army system rather than discouraging their substance abuse."

"Doesn't sound very rewarding," he offered.

"That's why I don't talk about it much," I said. "You and these guys that were here today made real sacrifices for their country. I chased pretty nurses around the burn center at Fort Sam. I was never deployed. Nothing was going on in the world at the time. Seeing what these guys gave up, I'm embarrassed about how little I contributed."

"You can't feel guilty because you never got sent to war," he said. "You volunteered. You served."

"Not like you did," I said. "It's why I want to help now, however I can."

"We always need volunteers at our headquarters," he said. "It's in Virginia."

"I'm in Florida, or the Bahamas, or the Caribbean," I said. "Not sure where I'll be in the near future. I'm going to give you what cash I have on me. I'll send more when I get back home."

"Any amount is appreciated," he said.

"How did you get involved with Enduring Warrior?" I asked.

"As a civilian, I no longer had the sense of belonging to something greater than myself," he said. "I looked for some way I could still contribute to our military mission and our veterans. I found Enduring Warrior. I do a couple things for them. First, I'm a team athlete. We help our vets through physical challenges like we had today. Our sole goal is to give our vets their confidence back and motivate them to strive to do more as part of their recovery."

"I saw it working here today," I said.

"We have a number of programs," he continued. "We have a hunting and mountaineering group. We have a sky dive program and a SCUBA program, which I help to run. Our first step is to get our guys open water SCUBA certified and then help them work through other certifications to achieve their personal goals. It's a real pleasure for me diving with them and helping them through the process."

"I dive a little," I said. "But I'm no pro and I only like warm water."

"Look us up if you come back up here in the summer months," he said.

"I've got this thing looming," I said. "I think I'll be doing quite of bit of traveling soon."

"Sorry we couldn't work out a way for you to contribute further," he said.

"I've got this one thought I don't want to leave hanging," I said. "There's this young Marine that I've mentored. I don't know where he is right now. He's kind of adrift. He's got no purpose in life but to hide from it. I've got a feeling I'll see him again. If I can talk him into heading your way, will you take him under your wing? He's a fine young man I assure you."

"I'll do what I can," he said.

"Ames," I said. "Daniel Ames. He'll tell you I sent him if he ever shows up. I don't want him to end up like me."

"You don't seem so bad," he said.

"If you only knew," I told him. "I'm going to let you get on with it. It's been a real pleasure talking with you. Thanks for all you do for our vets."

"Thank you for your service," he said. "Good luck to you."

As I drove back to the hotel, my mind switched back to Brody's predicament. Maybe I was being selfish, but was that wrong? Since the loss of my wife, I'd always been self-centered. Most of the time there was no one to count on but myself. Looking out for number one had been my means of survival. That started to change when Brody came into my life. We were staying in a marina so that she'd be comfortable. I would have preferred to be at anchor, but

I was willing to compromise to assure her happiness and comfort. I had to admit, living in a marina was a luxury compared to being anchored out.

Now, I wasn't just asking her to turn down a job offer, I was asking her to become a fugitive. It was too much to ask. I realized it then. I didn't want to lose her, but I would be preventing her from living a respectable life that she could be proud of. Instead, she'd be running and hiding for the rest of her life, hanging out with a boat bum with no future. I couldn't ask her to do it. As soon as I saw her I'd urge her to accept the offer and return to her former career. I'd be okay alone. I'd done it long enough. Maybe she could prevent them from coming after me if she worked for them. Maybe she could at least alert me, somehow, if they were on my trail. I wondered if she could ask them to leave me alone as part of her acceptance, negotiate on my behalf. Either way, my mind was made up. I'd have to let her go and disappear into the sunset once again. Sadness overtook me, but I wouldn't let it change my mind.

When I opened the door to the room, Brody came to me. She gave me a hug and whispered in my ear.

"The bags are packed," she said. "Let's get out of here, right now."

"Wait, Brody," I said. "I want you to take the job. I can't make you come with me."

"Bullshit," she said. "We're a team, damn it. Now let's roll. They probably had someone watch you drive in."

"You sure you've thought this through?" I asked.

"Including our travel arrangements," she said. "We'll ditch the car here. We'll get a cab to the airport. We'll split up and each buy multiple tickets to different destinations. We'll change planes several times in route to our final location. Take multiple cabs rides, constantly alert for a tail. We won't go back to the boat. We'll have someone bring it to us."

"I guess you have thought it through," I said. "Why not take separate cabs to different airports?"

"That's good," she said. "Keep thinking like that. Do not get followed to our meeting place."

"Which is where?" I asked.

"I was hoping for your input on that," she said. "You know the area better than I do. We'll have to have access to the boat when it arrives. We'll have to figure out who can bring it to us."

"Whoever gets to Punta Gorda first, gets a room at the Wyvern," I said. "Pay in cash. We'll take the tour boat out to Cayo Costa and meet up with *Miss Leap.* Our captain can take the tour boat back to Punta Gorda where someone will pick him up."

"Who's your first pick for captain?" she asked.

"Captain Lee on Evergreen," I suggested. "If not him maybe Mike and Moe would do it."

"I'll pick up a burner phone at the airport," she said. "I'll make the calls during layovers."

"Ditch the phone before you get to Florida," I said.

"They may have someone at the marina watching the boat," she said.

"They'll see a stranger drive it away," I said. "Have Captain Lee watch for a tail. Maybe go for a joy ride first, just to see if anyone is following."

"How will he warn us?"

"Use the flag at the stern," I said. "No flag means trouble and we abort. Flag flying means we're okay to meet."

"Sounds good," she said. "Are you ready for this?"

"Call the cabs," I said. "Leave that phone here."

Brody spent a few minutes writing down key contacts from her phone and put the list in her purse. I hadn't thought of it, but of course, I don't own a phone. She made the calls and we went out front to await our cabs. She was bound for Dulles and I was going to Reagan. When the first cab pulled up, we hugged and kissed goodbye.

"See you on the other side, Breeze," she said. "I love you."

"I love you too," I replied. "Be careful. It's going to be alright."

Then she was gone.

Five

I bought tickets to Denver, Salt Lake City, and Houston. At the last minute, I boarded the flight to Houston, mostly because it would be warm there. I had no clue where Brody was headed. I couldn't rat her out if I got caught. In Houston, I bought tickets for three more cities, settling on Atlanta as my destination. I sat in the airport and considered my options. One more flight and I'd be somewhere close to home. There had been no sign of any surveillance anywhere along the way. As far as I knew, I was a ghost. I went to the rental car counter, but they wanted a credit card. I didn't have one, and I wouldn't use it if I did. I thought about license plate readers, toll booths, credit card and ATM alerts. I'd have to avoid all of the tools that the FBI had at their disposal. Brody would know this too. I'd given her enough cash to see her through.

I booked a flight to Fort Lauderdale. I thought they might know enough to put someone at the Fort Myers airport. Tampa was too close to the marina. I still wasn't sure how I'd get to Punta Gorda. After I landed, I went outside to where the taxis, shuttles, and buses parked. I saw a car with an Uber sticker on the window.

"You want to make some real money today?" I asked the driver.

"What you need, man?" he asked.

"West coast, Punta Gorda," I said. "I'll pay in cash."

"That's three or four hours away, man," he said. "Then three or four hours back."

"What's it worth to you?" I asked.

"Eight hundred," he answered.

I peeled off eight big bills from the money roll in my pocket and handed it to him. He shrugged and told me to get in.

"You got an address, man," he said.

"Downtown," I said. "Don't put it in your GPS. I'll tell you how to get there."

"Lemme guess," he said. "I never gave you no ride, either."

"I'll give you two hundred more to forget you ever saw me," I offered.

"Easy money, man," he said. "You got a deal."

I did not think I was going too far to cover my tracks. I had to be absolutely certain that I wouldn't be found. The crucial time was from leaving Washington until we got our boat back. If we could make it to *Leap of Faith* undetected, we had a fighting chance to disappear forever. She would protect us.

I had the Uber driver drop me off a few blocks away from the Wyvern. There were three major hotels in Punta Gorda and several smaller motels. He couldn't know which one I was going to. I walked to the hotel and took the elevator to the top floor. I found Brody sitting at the rooftop bar.

"Hey, baby," I said. "Can you give a sailor a room for the night?"

"That's mighty bold of you, mister," she said. "But it's your lucky day. I've got a king-sized bed that needs filling."

"I'm your man," I said.

"I'm so happy to see you," she said. "How'd it go?"

"I'm in the clear," I said. "You?"

"So far, so good," she said. "I think I was more cautious than necessary."

"Me too," I confessed. "My paranoia knows no bounds."

"Don't stop now," she said. "We're almost there."

"Did you contact Captain Lee?"

"He said he'd do it," she said. "But he needs details from you."

"Did you get a new burner phone?"

"No, but there's a phone in the room," she said.

"Is it safe?"

"No way they could know what hotel we are in," she said. "Not yet anyway."

We went to the room and I called Lee.

"What have you got yourself into?" he asked.

"You don't need to know that," I answered.

"Well, I need to know exactly what it is you want me to do," he said.

"First, you can find the key in a coffee can in the lazarette," I told him. "When you back her out, she's going to walk to starboard. Keep the wheel hard over to port. Goose her a bit when you put her in forward. She'll start to spin, but you'll need to back up and go forward two or three times to get clear."

"I understand," he said.

"Keep her below seven knots," I said. "Go down to Charlotte Harbor and head no place in particular. Keep an eye out for someone following you."

"What if someone does?" He asked.

"Go up around Cape Haze," I instructed. "It's seven miles to marker five. Turn left until they can't see you. Make them come to you. Then you'll be certain they are following."

"Then what?"

"Bring her into Pelican Bay," I said. "If you have someone following, take down the flag on the stern. If you're alone, keep the flag flying."

"I got it," he said. "What do I do after that if I've got a tail? Take her back to the marina?"

"Go ahead and drop anchor," I said. "Keep an eye on them. They might give up and drop their surveillance if they see you settled in for the night."

"I don't want to stay out there all night," he said. "My wife will kill me."

"It's only two hours back to the marina," I said. "We'll see what happens. If you have to leave you'll have plenty of daylight left. Give it a few hours. The boat from here arrives at eleven."

"What time does it go back?"

"Three in the afternoon," I said. "If we're all clear, you'll need someone to pick you up at Fishermen's Village around five."

"What are you going to do if I have to go back to the marina?" he asked. "You'll be stranded out there."

"We can always rent a cabin," I said. "Take the ferry over to Pine Island, figure it out from there."

"The weather looks good for a boat ride," he said.

"We both really appreciate this, Lee," I said. "Sorry to put you out."

"I just hope it works," he said. "Good luck."

"Good luck to you, and thanks again.

We walked over to Fisherman's Village in plenty of time to catch the tour boat. They'd gotten a new one since I'd been there last. It was a double-decker job, top heavy and ugly. We took seats on the upper deck. As soon as it cleared the marina, I moved to the rear and stared out behind us. No one was following. I relaxed a little. Brody came and took the seat next to me, leaning in on my shoulder.

"Can you feel it yet?" I asked her.

"Feel what?"

"Freedom," I said. "It's just twenty miles down the harbor."

"How is running from the FBI freedom?" she asked, laughing.

"We'll be on the move," I told her. "You, me and *Miss Leap*, living on the sea. There will be no one to answer to, no one to tell us what to do."

"I've thought about all of this," she said. "You know I came this close to taking that job."

"I wouldn't have blamed you if you did," I said. "It would have hurt. I'd probably be a little mad, but I wouldn't have held it against you. It was the reasonable thing to do."

"Reasonable, responsible, and all that shit," she said.

"What changed your mind?"

"Breeze, most people live their entire lives without ever finding what we have," she said. "That's worth more than any career. I won't look back. I trust that you'll keep us safe."

"It'll work out," I said. "Shit always works out."

As we approached marker five, I saw *Leap of Faith* to our west. Captain Lee had come up and around Cape Haze to check for a tail. I could see no other boats on the harbor, which was a good sign.

"There she is," said Brody.

"I see her," I said. "She looks to be alone."

"I think we're going to make it," she said. "Have you figured out where to go next?"

"Away from here," I said. "We should leave tonight."

"Into the wild blue yonder," she said. "I'm with you, captain."

The tour boat dropped us off at the docks on Cayo Costa. We sat in the shade of a pavilion, waiting for Captain Lee and *Miss Leap.* An hour later, we saw him approach the entrance to the bay. He swung over close to the docks with the flag flying. I never appreciated the flag of the United States of America more than I did at that moment. Brody literally squealed with delight. Our ticket to ride had arrived, and the coast was clear.

We watched Lee lower the dinghy and head for the docks. He was smiling as he approached.

Brody grabbed a line and tied him off. I gave him a hand getting up on the dock.

"All is well I assume?" he asked.

"As long as you say that no one followed you," I said.

"Never saw a thing," he said. "Nothing suspicious around the marina. No boats behind me all morning."

"That's great news," said Brody. "We can't thank you enough."

"Let me pay you for your trouble," I said, pulling out my money roll.

"All I need is a ride back to the mainland," he said. "And maybe one of them Klondike bars while I wait for the boat to leave."

"You got it, captain," I said.

We told the tour boat captain that Lee would be taking our seats on the return trip. It wasn't a problem. The three of us sat and enjoyed Klondike bars before we departed. We said our goodbyes, and Brody and I took the dinghy out to see *Miss Leap.*

I patted her on the transom when we arrived at her stern.

"Good to see you, old girl," I said.

Brody jumped up over the transom, grabbed a big hunk of the boat and hugged it.

"We love you, *Miss Leap*," she said. "I'm sorry we ever left you."

"Check on our supplies," I said. "I'll see how much water we have."

We needed food and we needed water. The fuel was mostly full. I decided to leave immediately for Fort Myers Beach. We could stock up and get water in one day. I still had no other destination in mind, but I'd figure it out. We'd stay on the move until we got someplace safe, someplace it wasn't likely for the FBI to be.

We cruised down my favorite stretch of water and the old feelings came back to me. Once again, I was running from something that may not exist. It was completely possible that no effort had been made to locate Brody, not yet anyway. On the other hand, a boat full of G-men could have been waiting outside the bay to take us into custody. There was nothing I could do but keep chugging along at seven knots. It was a reasonable assumption that we were safe for the time being, but we couldn't hang around home waters for long. Sooner or later, they'd catch up to us.

The front mooring field was full, so we motored on. There on the back mooring field floated *Lion's Den*. Daniel was in town. I looked around for *Another Adventure*, but apparently, Holly wasn't there. I couldn't believe my eyes. I had a feeling that our paths would cross again, but I never expected it to be so soon.

Six

There was no dinghy tied to Daniel's boat. That meant he wasn't aboard. We watched the sun set and kept an eye out for him to return.

"So what was your route during our great escape?" asked Brody.

"Houston, Atlanta, and Fort Lauderdale," I answered.

"How did you get to Punta Gorda?"

"I hijacked an Uber driver at the airport," I said.

"That must have cost a fortune," she said.

"Yup," I said. "How about you?"

"I'd tell you but then I'd have to kill you," she said.

"Secret agent Brody," I said.

"I bought a motorcycle from some dude in Sarasota," she said. "He signed the title but I didn't. I left it at Laishley Park."

"You ride bikes?" I asked.

"It's been a while," she said. "But I felt very anonymous with a helmet on."

"Good work," I said.

We saw Daniel coming out from a canal. He saw *Leap of Faith* right away and came over to us.

"Hi guys," he said. "Fancy meeting you here. I was on my way to your marina."

"I guess we saved you the trip," I said. "What the hell are you doing here?"

Daniel climbed aboard. We shook hands and Brody got a hug.

"After the hurricane, Holly wanted to go back to the Keys to help out," he said. "Key West wasn't hit too bad, so we went up to Boot Key. She called some old friends from Tampa that had a bunch of dive gear and lift equipment and went to work. She was really something. Wouldn't take any money. Only helped those without insurance. Ten and twelve hour days."

"You were helping her weren't you?"

"Of course I was," he said. "But those other dudes really knew what they were doing. I was out of the circle, if you know what I mean. They were all friends and I was the stranger."

"You're gone for good?" asked Brody.

"It's just not going to happen for her and me as a couple," he said. "She's great and all, but it was time to move on."

"That's too bad," Brody said. "You were cute together."

"So why did you come looking for us?" I asked.

"I lost my free sailboat ride around the world," he said. "You're the only friends I have down here."

"I hate to break it to you," I said. "But we're out of here tomorrow and we don't want to be found."

"What happened?" he asked.

"In a nutshell," I said. "The FBI ordered Brody to go back to work. She chose not to. Now they may or may not be looking for us."

"As in hunt-you-down looking for you?"

"Maybe," I said. "It's a bunch of political crap. Brody knows things."

"Well, that sucks balls," he said. "Where you gonna go?"

"We don't even know yet," I told him.

"How will I get in touch with you?" he asked. "I tried Brody's number yesterday."

"We don't have a phone anymore," I said. "Give Brody your number so we can call if and when we get the chance."

"I was pretty psyched to see you two," he said. "Now I feel like I've been kicked in the ass."

"I'm sorry, Dan," I said. "I do have something I want to talk to you about."

Over beers, I told him about meeting the Marine Corps fighter pilot, Troy Warshel. I even confessed to my lame performance with the Enduring Warriors. I skipped the part about me taking blood pressure medication.

"Besides the hikes, they've got a hunting program and they teach wounded vets how to SCUBA dive," I said. "They even go skydiving."

"Man, that sounds right up my alley," he said. "I can do all that shit."

"I'd like for you to consider meeting Troy and some of the guys," I said. "I think there might be a place for you in the organization."

I saw his eyes light up just a little. I could see the wheels turning in his mind.

"Where is this place?" he asked.

"Troy lives in Maryland," I said. "But their office is in Virginia someplace."

"That was my turf," he said. "My sister lives up there."

"How in the world did you manage all this?" he asked.

"Just stumbled into it," I said. "Met him in a bar while Brody was getting grilled by the FBI Director."

"And you thought of me?" he asked.

"It became quite clear that I wasn't up to the task," I said. "I really wanted to help. I thought maybe you could pick up my slack."

"I appreciate you thinking about me," he said. "But you didn't even know where I was."

"Somehow, I thought I'd see you again," I said. "Don't know why, but here you are."

I gave him Troy's card. It felt like handing him a ticket to a purpose in life. I'd aided and abetted his desire to be a boat bum and avoid responsibility. Now I was trying to lead him back towards a meaningful life. It felt right.

"I'm going to call him," he said. "This is just what I needed. I've been thinking about something like this ever since I talked to that other vet you sent me too."

"Glad I could be of assistance," I said. "Troy knows your name. He promised to look out for you."

"You always seem to know what to do," he said.

"Sorry the Holly thing didn't work out," I said.

"No need to be sorry," he said. "The sailing was awesome. Holly is the queen of the ocean out there. She really knows how to make that boat sing. I learned a lot. Saw some cool places."

"Did you get enough?" I asked.

"It was a good experience," he said. "Meeting you and Brody, getting my own boat, sailing with Holly, meeting Jonnie Gee. All of this has really cleared my mind. Steered me in the right direction."

"It'll work out, kid," I said. "Shit works out."

"I'm starting to believe you," he said. "I'll be sad to see you go."

"If you need any help while you're here," I said. "Diver Dan is back there on that boat. Robin is over there on that little sailboat. Both of them are out here diving most every day."

"I've got a feeling I'll be heading north soon," he said. "After I talk to Troy."

"Good luck to you," I said. "Now give Brody a real hug."

Brody had tears in her eyes as they hugged. So did Daniel.

"You're a fine young man, Daniel Ames," she said. "We'll both miss you terribly."

"Take care of the old man," he said. "Get in touch when you can."

I hadn't felt like an old man when I'd left Guatemala. I'd been quick and strong. I'd still had it. Something happened over the past year or so. My attempts to reconcile my actions had been taxing on my soul. Living the luxurious marina life had made me soft. I drank too much and exercised too little. I'd been forced to take pills.

Maybe going on the run would be good for me. Maybe it would sharpen me up, both mentally and physically. I looked at Brody. She looked much younger than I. I was fifty-five years old and clearly mortal. I couldn't get old yet. There was still much life to live with her, assuming we could manage to avoid the FBI.

We watched Daniel drive away in the dark. I held Brody as she cried softly. It was just the three of us now; Brody, *Leap*, and me.

We sat in silence for a few minutes, until Brody spoke.

"Okay, captain," she said. "What do we do now?"

"Let me pick your brain for a minute," I said. "Tell me how the FBI will go about finding us."

"Assuming they are even looking for me," she said.

"Assume it's a full court press," I said. "All hands on deck. High priority."

"If they were watching the hotel, they saw us leave in separate taxis," she began. "They may have followed one or both of us. If not, they have CCTV, license plate readers, toll booths, and the like. They'd know we went to the airports in short order."

"Did our ticket buying deception do us any good?" I asked.

"Only temporarily," she said. "It's what we needed to do if they were hot on our trail. They'd see we bought three tickets. They'd compare them to the actual flight manifest and figure out where we went. Then again, and again, until our final stop. Each leads to the marina eventually."

"Captain Lee reported no suspicious activity at the marina," I said.

"He's not exactly a trained operative," she said. "But having him pilot our boat would have confused anyone who was looking. They wouldn't know what to think or where he was going."

"Could they commandeer a boat?" I asked.

"Not likely," she said. "And Lee said no one followed him. We got out of Pelican Bay undetected as far as we know."

"What do they do next?"

"Set up all the alerts," she said. "ATMs and banks, cell phone towers, cameras and all that good spy shit."

"Which we won't trigger," I said. "No phones, no ATM or credit cards, no car. Unless we run afoul of the law they simply won't find us. Will they put agents down here in pursuit?"

"It depends on how important it is to find me," she said. "I'd put two men in a fast boat. I'd send them out to Pelican Bay and down here looking. Known hangouts. We can't stay here."

"Groceries and water first thing in the morning," I said. "Then we cut and run."

"Where to?"

"If they were intensely searching for us, how long would the pressure stay on?"

"A week or two at the most," she said. "It would be a goose chase that they couldn't waste resources on for long."

"If we can hide someplace where they'd never find us for a few weeks, then we could move about more freely."

"What place would that be?"

"The Everglades," I said.

"I was afraid you were going to say that," she said. "Better stock up on bug spray."

"I can't see a couple of G-men going deep into the swamp looking for us," I said. "We sit way up in there for as long as we can, then we decide where to go next."

"You're right," she said. "They won't find us there."

"Now, what is your personal feeling about the depths of their desire to bring you in?" I asked her.

"It seemed important enough when I was sitting at the table with the FBI Director," she said. "But he's got to have his hands full with this Mueller investigation. Mike Flynn and all that."

"What happened with Flynn?" I asked.

"Mueller pinned him with a process crime," she said.

"What's that mean?"

"Flynn was on board with Trump's candidacy early on. They knew he would be the National Security Advisor if Trump won. After the election, Flynn spoke with a Russian Ambassador, among others. A new president can't just show up on inauguration day and start to work. He has to be brought up to speed before his inauguration. That's why we have the transition period."

"So that was a crime?" I asked.

"No, it wasn't," she said. "Mueller calls Flynn in and grills him. Does it again a few weeks later, then one more time. His investigators go through the transcripts and they see some discrepancies in his statements. He said he had not met with the Russian ambassador when he clearly did."

"Why would he do that?"

"I don't know," she said. "Maybe he thought it was a crime, even though it wasn't. The only crime is lying to the FBI."

"So no crime was committed," I said. "The FBI questions you and catches you in a lie. Your only problem arose due to the investigation, which otherwise found no crime?"

"That's about it," she said. "It's weak sauce for Mueller. It's got nothing to do with any collusion with the Russians by the Trump campaign. He was already president-elect when this took place."

"I don't have a scorecard," I said. "Is Flynn one of the good guys?"

"He was great as a General," she said. "Top notch, especially when it came to intelligence. He was a fine pick for National Security Advisor."

"But now he's gone and in deep shit," I said.

"He didn't last a month," she said. "Trump went with another General, McMaster. He rightfully decided to surround himself with military men. He knows little about foreign affairs."

"I still don't see why they would reach so far as to take out Flynn," I said. "Seems awfully petty in the scheme of things."

"Here's where it gets tricky," she said. "Flynn has always been known as a right-wing guy. Obama picked him to run the Defense Intelligence Agency anyway."

"Why?"

"The military is its own Deep State," she explained. "It's a military position and they decide who fills it. Flynn was admired by the military. He had all the credentials. He was the best man for the job at the time, but he opposed Obama's policies. Obama was his boss. When he spoke out publicly calling Obama weak and ineffectual, he was forced out."

"What's that got to do with the FBI?" I asked.

"Mueller, Comey, and their buddies are all leftists," she said. "They were loyal to Obama. Comey was especially loyal to Hillary Clinton. The Justice Department and the various intelligence agencies are all branches of the Democratic Party."

"So Flynn got taken down because he was a right-winger?"

"The military is less open about their political allegiances," she explained. "It's their own omerta. Top brass are to remain silent on politics and do their job regardless of who is in the White House or who controls the legislature. This unwritten rule extends into retirement. Flynn became more and more vocal when he was working for Trump. He went hardcore conservative."

"So the left-wing FBI shut him up."

"And a petty process crime was all they could come up with," she said. "He must be squeaky clean otherwise. Show me the man and I'll show you the crime. They had to reach way out there for Flynn."

"How does this influence the current FBI Director?" I asked. "He's the one who'll call the shots as far as we're concerned."

"He won't want any more embarrassment for the Company," she said. "Comey left behind a mess. His bumbling of the Hillary investigation won't soon be forgotten."

"You know I don't pay any attention to this stuff," I said. "What was that all about?"

"Hillary is guilty as hell for all sorts of wrongdoing," she explained. "But Comey, being the good soldier, dutifully covered it up. He made a fool of himself in the process. Everyone knew he'd never recommend charges to the DOJ, but he gets up there and calls her careless and stupid. He invents new law by saying she didn't have any intent to do harm and lets her off the hook. Then the infamous tarmac meeting between Bill and Loretta Lynch goes down. Everyone knew what that was all about, but there was Comey, taking it like a clown in a dunking booth. He besmirched the office and the Bureau as a whole. After the fact, he wanted to punish whoever blew the whistle on the meeting. It was all a big stinking pile."

"I'm trying to understand how this affects us," I said. "This Chris Wray had to be careful not to allow any more scandal at the FBI. What is scandalous about your separation?"

"Looking back, I think taking a leave of absence after being exonerated for the shooting wasn't a good idea," she said. "I became obsessed with finding you, thinking I could take you back as a trophy. That I'd get back in their good graces with my fine investigative work. Then I fell in love with you and that plan went out the window."

"I'm glad it did," I said. "But I'd been cleared somewhere along the line. Why'd you keep looking?"

"I had to win the game I was playing with myself," she said. "I had to prove to myself that I could find you."

"So what is it that you know, that the FBI wants to keep quiet?"

That was the million dollar question. What did she know? Was it valuable enough for them to pursue her? Would we be safe from surveillance in a few weeks, or would they hound us forever? If they found us, would they bring us in for questioning, or would they simply put a bullet in our heads? I had ignored politics for a very long time. It simply didn't interest me. I didn't have health insurance. I didn't pay taxes. I didn't even have a phone. Whoever was in charge and whatever laws they passed had no impact on me. Suddenly, it had become quite personal. Washington had reached down into the backwaters of Florida to lay a hand on me, via Brody. I thought her aborted career in the FBI would be useful to our pursuits. Instead, it might have been the cause of our death warrants.

"What do you know, Brody?" I asked again.

"That the FBI worked closely with the Clinton camp on talking points concerning her email server. That the FBI knows what's on that server and it's criminal. That the FBI helped to legitimize the supposed pissing dossier knowing full well that it was a complete fabrication. That it was used to get a FISA warrant to surveil team Trump, then unmask any American that got caught up in their eavesdropping. That's how they got Manafort indicted."

"Who is Manafort?"

"He worked on Trump's transition team," she said. "They found some old financial transactions that weren't reported, long before he worked for Trump. Meanwhile, Hillary's campaign director failed to report far worse dealings with foreign powers. They knew, but failed to press charges."

"Hillary's campaign director?"

"Podesta," she said. "He got paid by companies that were partially or wholly owned by the Russian government. Not a crime, but failing to report is. Manafort worked for the Ukranian government, which is not part of Russia, but pro-Kremlin."

"I told you I didn't have a scorecard," I said. "Sounds like everybody was playing footsie with Russia except Trump himself."

"He's had business dealings with them," she said. "But nothing to do with the election. The whole conspiracy was drummed up by Podesta himself."

"Where's Podesta now?"

"He's totally off the radar," she said. "I couldn't tell you if he's hiding or if he's dead."

"I don't like the sound of that," I said. "Maybe we should leave here tonight."

"We need food," she said. "And water."

"How'd you manage to get in so deep?" I said. "How do you know all this stuff?"

"Everyone at the FBI knows," she said. "Comey corrupted the FBI beyond your wildest imagination, all for political purposes due to his association with the Clintons."

"They can't keep everyone quiet, can they?"

"It's part of the fabric of the Company," she said. "The Company first. Code of silence. Code of honor."

"It doesn't sound honorable to the best interests of the country," I said.

"Company first, country second."

In one conversation we'd covered General Flynn, Hillary Clinton, James Comey, and Donald Trump. Then there was me. Which one of these things was not like the others?

"Damn, Brody," I said. "Just damn. We can get water tonight. We'll stop in Marco for food. Better get cracking."

"I'm sorry, Breeze," she said. "Tell me it's going to be okay."

"It'll work out," I said. "Now let's get moving."

Seven

We filled water jugs at the dinghy dock and hauled them back to fill the boat tanks. It took three trips. It was late and we were tired. I managed one beer for a nightcap before calling it quits. I wanted to go to bed, but night travel was on the schedule instead.

We dodged stone crab traps for six hours before making Capri Pass into Marco. It was tedious in the dark, but we had a good moon. I made the tricky right into Collier Creek and we weaved our way into Smokehouse Bay. I didn't prefer to anchor there, but there was a grocery store with easy access for the dinghy. We didn't talk. We didn't make love. We just hit the sack and quickly fell asleep.

The morning light came too soon. I dragged Brody out of bed and handed her a cup of coffee. We got our provisions before eight in the morning. I fired up the engine while Brody put things away. We had a nine hour run to Little Shark River. After an hour or so more crawling upriver, we'd find a good hideaway. If the FBI found us there, so be it. I could think of no better place on Earth to go. Dealing with the mosquitoes and alligators would be better than dealing with a government hitman.

I went further up the Little Shark River than I'd ever gone. I passed the spot where I'd tracked down a thief and recovered stolen money. He took a shot at me with a spear gun. After he missed, the confrontation was over quickly. I wasn't old then. I was bold and decisive. I willed the events to turn out in my favor. The little bastard didn't have a chance.

I eased *Leap of Faith* into Oyster Bay. It was barely deep enough for our four-foot draft. Behind an unnamed island, I discovered a small cove, just big enough for us. I dropped the anchor and backed in towards the mangroves. I wanted to put our stern far enough under cover that our name couldn't be read from the air. I asked Brody to prepare a stern anchor.

"Why don't we just tie off to the mangroves?" she asked.

"No point in giving the swamp critters an easy way on board," I said.

"What kind of swamp critters?"

"Big snakes, rats, spiders," I said.

"That sounds pleasant," she said. "How bad is it going to suck to be here for a couple weeks?"

"I'm more concerned with the mosquitoes," I told her. "Let's get everything without a screen closed up. Break out the spray."

We settled into our hiding place, deep in the Everglades. It had a prehistoric feel to it. There were no humans within fifty miles of us. There were no sounds from cars or air traffic. It was beautiful and dangerous at the same time. There was no real land to set foot on. It was all muck and mangroves. It was home to several species of venomous snakes, including rattlers, coral snakes, and cottonmouths. Over the years, the python population had exploded. They weren't native to the area, but they thrived. There were plenty of gators there as well. We wouldn't be leaving the boat, except to fish in the dinghy.

Long before sunset, we heard them coming. A mosquito scout had spotted us, rounded up several million of his buddies, and led them to our hideout. A dark cloud appeared over the bay. A million buzzing demons flew in formation towards us. I sprayed a strong DEET concoction around the doorways and on the window screens. We retreated indoors as the cloud descended upon us.

"Jesus Christ, Breeze," said Brody. "Look at them."

The windows were black with bugs. I pulled down the blinds so we didn't have to look at them. I handed Brody a flyswatter.

"If you see one in here kill it immediately," I said. "Before he tells his friends how he got inside."

"You sure know how to show a girl a good time," Brody said.

We went through the same drill every afternoon for two weeks. It was not a good time. With the hatches and doors closed, the inside temperature was in the nineties. Tucked in the way we were, no breeze could reach us. We both smelled of pits and ass. We couldn't waste too much water for bathing. We took whore baths and used up all the wet wipes trying to keep our odor to a minimum. We couldn't jump overboard unless we were up to wrestling alligators. We didn't run out of food, but we did run out of books to read. There was no television to watch. It was a miserable existence, but no G-men came calling.

One morning I noticed a west wind up above the trees. I got an idea.

"Grab a bathing suit," I told Brody. "We're going for a dinghy ride."

"Where to?" she asked.

"The beach," I said. "Pack some dish soap too."

"Is it safe?" she asked.

"We'll poke our nose out into the Gulf and see," I said. "We can get cleaned up without getting eaten."

"What about sharks?" she asked. "It's probably not called Shark River for nothing."

"Stay in the shallow water," I instructed. "I'll keep watch while you bathe. Then you can keep a lookout for me."

"You just want to see me naked," she said.

"Incidental perk," I argued. "Neither of us smells pretty. It's time to do something about that. The west wind will keep the bugs inshore."

"A bath with no bugs," she said. "Thank God for small miracles."

I threw an extra gas can in the dinghy and turned on my handheld GPS. It'd be easy to get lost in the maze of turns and tunnels. We worked our way back down the river, seeing no one. We took a shortcut to Ponce de Leon Bay, which had a small strip of sand facing the Gulf. I beached the dinghy and drug it up into some tall seagrass. The water was tannin stained, but clear. It was just cool enough to be refreshing. There were no boats or planes in sight. I kept an eye out for shark fins while Brody got cleaned up. Dish soap works well in salt water, even for shampoo. Brody reveled in cleaning herself. I reveled in watching.

We switched places, keeping an eye on the water and the sky. We were alone. It felt good to swish soap suds over my body. I wanted to take a little swim but thought better of it. No point in staying exposed for too long. When we got back on board we rinsed off with fresh water and put on some clean clothes. We applied deodorant and Brody sprayed some air freshener around the salon. We were cleaned and we smelled good.

"I never once bought air freshener until you came along," I said.

"When I saw you for the first time, in that bar in Fort Myers Beach," she said. "You were clean shaven and freshly showered like this."

"I'd just taken my first shower in weeks," I admitted. "They've got great showers there. Worth the price of a mooring ball."

"You weren't what I'd expected," she said. "I had this picture in my mind of some crusty hermit who'd managed to evade the FBI by hiding in a place like this. I'd thought you'd look like Tom Hanks in Castaway. Eating turtles to survive. Licking toads for kicks."

"For the record," I said. "I've never licked a toad. I have, however, let myself go when there were no women to impress."

"Who were you there to impress that day?" she asked.

"The bartender, Jennifer," I said. "The first thing she tells me is that she has a boyfriend and he's sitting right there. The second was that an FBI agent was looking for me."

"You managed to keep your composure," she said. "You never flinched."

"It was a surprising turn of events," I admitted. "But looking at it now, it was clearly serendipitous."

"We've been great together, haven't we?" she said. "It's been a great ride, up until now."

"But even now, you aren't bitching," I said. "This sucks but you're taking it calmly. Not complaining."

"Oh I'd like to complain," she said. "I'd like to complain about the goddamn mosquitoes, the sea of sweat, eating canned food, the isolation, the not knowing what's going on out there or what our future holds. But it's all my fault. I got us into this. I'm the reason we're holed up here."

"We'll have to leave here soon," I told her. "We're running low on bug spray."

"Where do we go?"

"Not sure," I said. "It sure would be nice to know if they were still looking for us."

"I don't know how we can find that out," she said. "Anyone I still know up there is neck deep in the swamp. They wouldn't tell me anything when I called the first time. They're going to keep their heads down and not get involved in this. Might even rat me out."

I thought better with a beer in my hand, so I grabbed a cold one from the fridge. We were low on beer too. It was definitely time to go.

How could we find out what was going on with the FBI and Brody? Who did I know that could help, without giving us up? We'd ditched the phone and Brody's tablet. We'd been completely out of touch for over two weeks. Until we could verify that there was no active chase, we'd have to continue living like this. We both wanted out of the Everglades, and we needed supplies sooner or later.

"How do those burner phones work?" I asked her.

"You buy a dirt cheap phone at a convenience store," she said. "Put thirty minutes of talk on it and throw it away after you make your call. Good spies destroy the SIM card too."

"It can't be traced?"

"It's an anonymous purchase," she said. "You only use it once. That's the point."

"So if we go to town somewhere, we could get a call out?"

"Who you gonna call?" she asked.

"I know a guy in D.C," I said. "We've already sent an envoy to meet him."

"Daniel?"

"Yes, Daniel was going to meet Troy Warshel," I said. "He should be settled in up there by now."

"Troy," she said. "The Enduring Warrior guy."

"Right. He's a Marine," I said. "He was a fighter pilot. Now works for the Department of Defense. He's in and out of the White House and the Pentagon all the time."

"He's got to know somebody who knows or can find out what's going on," she said.

"Exactly."

"Do you have his number?" she asked.

"No, I gave his card to Daniel," I said.

"But I've got Daniel's number," she said. "We can call Daniel to get word to this Troy guy."

"How will they get back to us?"

"We toss the first phone," she explained. "Then call back on another phone a few days later. The messages will have to be short and not explanatory. Just a quick no current search, or search still on."

"We need to be somewhere secure in the meantime," I said. "Keep our current protocols in place until we have some breathing room."

"Is there anywhere along this coast that you've never been?" she asked. "Someplace with no known connection to you?"

"Naples," I said. "I've never stopped there even for one night. It's big enough for us to stay in the shadows. Find a phone and do our thing. No one knows me there."

"Naples it is," she said. "Can we leave soon? This place is killing me."

"Let's check the weather and make ready to pull anchor," I said. "We'll move in the dark, anchor off the coast until morning."

Eight

We forgot to shut the cabin door while we pulled up anchor that night. We picked up a horde of fanged, flying stowaways as we cruised down the river. After anchoring outside of Gordon Pass off the coast of Naples, they set upon us the instant we went below. It was a small army, but a vicious one. DEET was sprayed and fly swatters were deployed in a frenzied fight. It was touch and go at first, but we eventually got the upper hand. Small blood spatters dotted the ceiling. Those that escaped were flying into Naples, looking for blood elsewhere.

"Nothing like carrying a memento of our cruise back with us," said Brody. "Let's never go back there again."

"Let's hope we have no reason to," I said.

I studied the chart to see what Naples held for us. Naples Bay would put us in the downtown area. There were several marinas, but I wasn't sure if we could check in without giving up our identity. It was my impression that anchoring was frowned upon. I didn't want to attract a visit from marine patrol. I didn't have enough knowledge of the area to make a decision. We'd have to wing it.

We got some rest while waiting for the sun to come up. It rose big and bright over the condos that lined the shore. We decided to treat ourselves to breakfast ashore. While motoring up the bay, I noticed two sailboats anchored northwest of marker twelve among a row of beautiful homes. I figured if it was okay for them, it would be okay for us. We dropped our hook a respectful distance from them and lowered the dinghy.

We found a city pier in the center of the downtown area. It was a short walk to any number of restaurants. It felt eerie walking amongst the general public after so much isolation. My head was on a swivel, watching people and looking for anything out of the ordinary. I noticed Brody doing it too. We were hyper-aware of our surroundings.

After breakfast, we bought a phone. We found a quiet place to call Daniel. I listened as Brody explained our predicament. She asked him to relay the information to Troy. We hoped that Troy could tell us something. She told Daniel to erase the call from his phone log and not to call back on that number. She promised to call him from another number in two days. After she hung up, I removed the SIM card and snapped the phone in half. I put one half in a nearby trash can. The other half went into a trash can a few blocks away. On the way back to the boat, I tossed the SIM card overboard. The first step towards getting much-needed information had been taken.

We spent the next few days cleaning up the boat and getting groceries. I saw no way to get water except to go to a fuel dock. I knew most of them wanted you to buy fuel in order to get water. We didn't really need diesel, but I pulled into a fuel dock anyway. We took only forty gallons, but we were able to fill the water tanks and dispose of our trash. If we needed to run, the boat was ready for another extended trip.

We bought another phone and Brody called Daniel again. Troy wanted us to call him directly. He had some information. Brody asked Daniel to tell Troy to expect a call from a strange number that afternoon. We destroyed that phone and SIM card and walked around downtown. Later in the afternoon, we bought our third burner phone.

"Troy, this is Breeze," I said.

"Holy crap, buddy," he said. "What have you gotten yourself into?"

"It's a long story," I said. "But my girl Brody and I are on the run, specifically from the FBI."

"I'm not positive," he said. "But maybe you can relax a little bit."

"They didn't launch an all-out search for us?"

"They did at first," he said. "They sent a bunch of guys to your neck of the woods. Wray was absolutely livid. I'm surprised they didn't find you."

"Are they still looking?"

"Brody was all the buzz for a few days," he said. "A wildcard that Wray couldn't afford to have running loose."

"But something changed," I said. "What happened?"

"Oh it's bad," he said. "Brody would understand better. Let me talk to her."

We were alone so she put the phone's speaker on so I could hear.

"I don't want to get you into trouble," Brody said. "Who are you talking to up there?"

"My guy's in military intelligence with every possible security clearance," he explained. "He's dialed into Mueller's team and the FBI. He's getting a kick out of it."

"What's the big news that threw me off the front pages?" she asked.

"Mueller's lead investigator turns out to be an anti-Trump douchebag," he said. "He was cheating on his wife and sent dubious text messages to his mistress."

"What kind of dumbass uses texting when he knows everyone is being watched and listened to? What kind of stuff did he send?"

"Stupid, right?" he said. "He sent rabid anti-Trump and pro-Hillary messages. This is the same guy who showed up at the White House and grilled Flynn without a lawyer present. Flynn didn't even know he was being investigated. This is the same guy that interviewed Hillary, with no swearing in, no transcripts or recording whatsoever."

"Who was it?" asked Brody.

"Peter Strzok," he said.

"He was always a dickhead," she said.

"Now he's dickhead non-grata," said Troy. "Mueller demoted him to HR."

"He sent him to the dungeon?"

"He should have fired him, but he knows too much damaging stuff," said Troy. "Hillary, Huma, and several aids were all given a pass by this dude, but he's trying to nail Flynn on far less. It really looks bad. Plus Mueller hid the information from Congress until now, in spite of subpoenas requesting documents specifically mentioning Strzok."

"What's Wray doing while all of this is going down?"

"Get this," he said. "He sent a memo to all FBI employees trying to boost morale. He urged them to act with honor and integrity in everything they do."

"Seems a little late for that now," she said. "So what happened to the pursuit of me and Breeze?"

"It simply fell off the radar," he said. "There's been no chatter at all. I can't say for certain what's going on. I suppose he's hoping that you don't surface and add more misery to his plate."

"Is there any way we could tell him just that?" she asked. "Assure him that I'll keep my mouth shut?"

"I don't know, Brody," he said. "I could send it through channels, but I'm not sure it will do any good. If he wants you burned, he won't stop until he gets your charred corpse."

"I hate to ask," she said. "But try to find out for sure. I'll call again in a few days. Won't be from this number."

"Keep your head down," he said. "Stay safe."

"I didn't like the sound of that charred corpse comment," I said. "Surely they can't afford another scandal centered on you. They won't try to take us out will they?"

"If they can't quietly assassinate me, they can make up any story they want as to why they had to take me out. Rogue agent gone bad or something. Play themselves as heroes for cleaning house."

"Seems like too much heat is on them to me," I speculated. "You've got to be small potatoes to them right now."

"Can we afford to take that chance?" she asked.

"No, I guess not," I answered. "Maybe Troy will have better news when we call him next."

The boat was full of fuel and water. We picked up some more groceries and bug spray, just in case. We looked for bars that had the news on TV to try to glean any information we could. There was an inkling of the things Troy had mentioned here and there. We heard Strzok's name mentioned several times. Over the next two days, we heard more names. Brody knew the players. Jeannie Rhee was also on Mueller's team. She'd been the personal attorney for Ben Rhodes, Obama's Deputy National Security Advisor. She also worked for the Clinton Foundation. More news outlets picked up on the story and started checking into the rest of Mueller's handpicked henchmen.

We went to the library so Brody could get some computer time. She learned that the entire team was staffed with Clinton loyalist and Democratic operatives. All of them had donated heavily to major Democratic campaigns, including Obama and Hillary. Strzok had been the lead FBI investigator on the Russian collusion theory since before Mueller was named as Special Counsel. He'd signed the documents creating the new investigation. He'd been the one who changed the wording of Comey's statement on Hillary's private server.

He changed "grossly negligent" to "extremely careless", which lessened the legal implications.

I didn't know anything about all of this, but Brody explained it to me the best she could. It certainly appeared that finding her wouldn't be a top priority. The FBI was under intense scrutiny. They couldn't afford any missteps. Still, we were not at liberty to move about freely. We'd been in one spot for too long already.

When we called Troy again, we got no answer. Seconds later we got a text.

Call your other friend. Can't talk. Do it now.

We had no time to exchange phones yet again. Brody called Daniel right away.

"He thinks his phone traffic has been monitored," Daniel said. "They know he got a call from Naples. You need to get out of there right away."

"Any word on my situation?" Brody asked.

"We just don't know," he said. "Either way. No one's talking about you and everyone is paranoid about what they say or who they say it to. You might be forgotten, or Wray has put the thing underground."

"Okay," she said. "I've got to hang up. I'll call again at some point. Answer strange numbers."

"Bye," was all he said.

Naples had been burned for us. The Everglades was simply too uninviting to return to so soon. We were ready for travel, but I was at a loss as to where to go.

"Bahamas again?" asked Brody.

"If we check in, our passports will raise a red flag at the State Department," I said. "Trust me, I know."

"What if we don't check in?" she asked.

"I've done it before," I said. "There is no enforcement, but if you need anything at all, the first thing they want is your cruising permit."

"Can we make do without one?" she asked. "What could happen that would require us to need it?"

"Parts mainly," I explained. "If the boat breaks down we'd need it to get parts. We can do without some stuff, but the motor has to run."

"Can we carry spares?"

"It's just not feasible to have a spare for everything that might fail," I said. "Plus we'd need time to buy them, and a place to ship them to."

"We can't dawdle around," she said. "We need to pick a place and go. What about Mexico?"

"I imagine it's tough to stay there without showing your passport," I said.

"Where in the U.S. could we go and stay hidden?" she asked.

"Texas? Louisiana?" I suggested. "The East Coast seems too close to Washington, and Florida."

"Do we stay on the move or do we find some little town and try to blend in?" she asked. "Or maybe a big city would be better."

"I wouldn't last long in a big city," I said. "But in a small town word gets around. Folks would ask questions."

"I'm thinking that every time we move, we risk exposing ourselves to someone who recognizes the boat. We need to hole up away from prying eyes, but please not in the Everglades."

"Then let's hop over to the Bahamas," I said. "We'll risk needing parts. If something happens to the boat, I'll figure it out."

"Are we going to cross Lake O?" she asked. "It'll be much quicker than swinging through the Keys."

"The lock operators log every boat that goes through," I told her. "If someone was smart, they'd be checking on that. Just as good as a toll booth camera or license plate reader."

"I wasn't aware of that," she said. "The Keys it is."

We trashed the last cheap phone and prepared to get underway. We could pick up another one in the Bahamas eventually. We wouldn't have access to good weather resources, but we'd have to make do. We could always get the National Weather Service forecasts on the VHF.

"Here we go again, *Miss Leap*," I said to our old boat. "We're counting on you, girl."

During our recovery from the hurricane, I'd gone over nearly every part of the engine. Our battery bank was brand new. The oil had been changed. The fuel filters were new. She was as ready to cruise as she would ever be. All of the precautions we'd taken in order to avoid the FBI had not been in vain. They had indeed been looking for us, but we'd escaped detection. We'd hoped to learn that the chase had been called off, but that didn't happen. We could be reasonably sure that someone would show up in

Naples. After that, we had no way of knowing if anyone would pursue us further.

Floating off an empty beach in the Bahamas was far preferable to fighting off mosquitoes in the Everglades. We'd have to trust that *Leap* wouldn't let us down. It wouldn't be the first time I'd depended on her to take care of me. I thought of the places I'd been. I really liked the Berry Islands. I thought Hoffman's Cay would be a nice place to settle in for an extended stay. We could pick up supplies in Great Harbor, but we'd have to go to Chub Cay for water. The water at Great Harbor Cay was not drinkable. Bottled water was hard to find and quite expensive. We could last indefinitely amongst the islands of the Berry chain.

Nine

As a political agnostic, I had a hard time fathoming how politics were now impacting my life. When the FBI had come looking for me in the past, it was because of my actions. I deserved to be hunted. This time, it was because of Brody's actions, or inaction, but did she deserve to be hunted? All I ever wanted was for the government to leave me alone. Brody had gone to work for them, and her circumstances had led to our current situation. The government seemed to hold way too much power over our lives as a result. That couldn't be a good thing, no matter which side of the political aisle one sat. The surveillance tools at the government's disposal were being used for political purposes. Brody had gotten caught up in that unintentionally. It was my problem too. We were a team. She could have solved her situation simply by returning to her job. She'd chosen me, fully aware of the consequences. I didn't take her choice lightly.

It was up to me to keep us out of harm's way until some future solution could be reached. We would flee together. We would run. It was something I was good at. We turned *Leap of Faith* south and ran down the coast past Marco. We veered out around the Cape Romano Shoals and made a course for the old Yacht Channel that cut across Florida Bay. We ran in the dark through the narrow channel. Brody manned the spotlight to help me find the few markers that remained after the hurricane. Finally, we anchored behind the Lorelei in Islamorada.

The next day we got lunch at the bar and watched the news. I wanted to catch the weather report, but we both had one ear cocked for any news out of the ongoing debacle in Washington. There was no mention of Brody's name. Various important people were calling for Mueller to resign. Others called for an investigation into the investigators. Leaks out of the White House suggested that Trump was planning to form his own spy group to counter the existing bias in our current agencies.

The weather forecast was a good one.

We made our way further up the Keys and staged inside Angelfish Creek. The mechanical voice on the VHF assured me that the weather was right for crossing the Gulf Stream. Other vessels in our vicinity were bound for Bimini. We were bound for Gun Cay. Anyone stopping in Bimini would be expected to check in with Immigration immediately. There was nothing at Gun.

The weather was not right for crossing the Gulf Stream, at least not at first. We found six-foot seas once we cleared the reef. It made for an unpleasant ride. Brody gave me dirty looks. It got worse in the center of the Stream. I debated with myself on whether or not we should turn back. Paranoia ruled my choice. We needed to keep running. We sloshed through it until the seas began to subside. The waves lessened. The further we got from the center of the Stream the calmer it became. By mid-afternoon, we cruised across a glass calm ocean. The water was a deep cobalt blue.

"This is more like it," said Brody. "It's beautiful."

"The weather guy said it would be calm," I said. "He just didn't specify when."

We anchored behind Gun Cay with no other boats in sight. I put up the quarantine flag for the night. There was no reason to be alert for FBI agents in that place. We relaxed and got a good night's sleep for the first time in a long time.

We left before sunup to cross the Bahama Banks. We encountered few boats along the way. The ones we did see were bound for Chub or Nassau. No one else was going to the Berry's. It took every minute of daylight to reach Bullock's Harbor on Great Harbor Cay. We had no reason to go ashore there. We had everything we needed on board. I raised the Bahamas courtesy flag before we approached the anchorage. Everyone would assume that we'd already checked in at Bimini, or elsewhere.

We departed the next day. Our course took us up around Big and Little Stirrup Cays, then south on the Atlantic side of Great Harbor. I brought us back inshore to pick up the shallow draft inside route. I slowed and checked the tide. It was low, and that was a bad thing. I'd been too hasty to get underway and our timing was off. We were about to run out of water.

I slowed even more and tried to read the water. I stayed in the darker blue areas and crawled along. Brody was on the bow shouting instructions. She looked nice up there in her bikini. I made a mental note to resume our sex life as soon as possible. All of the fear and drama had put a dent in our lovemaking. Boom, we hit something hard. The depth finder read six feet. It must have been a rock or a piece of coral. I couldn't go any slower and still maintain steerage. We inched along at three knots until we ran aground on soft sand.

There was a bit of a chop on the water due to an east wind. The boat was still in gear. I felt a wave pick us up and we moved forward a few feet before settling back down on the sand. I looked at Brody and shrugged. Another wave came and we gained another few feet. I left the boat in gear. We managed to leapfrog several more times until we regained deeper water.

The anchorage at Hoffman's Cay was empty. We picked a spot about a hundred yards off the prettiest little beach Brody had ever seen. She wanted to go to that beach immediately. I just wanted to sit and enjoy the surroundings, and a cold beer.

"You are taking me to that beach," she said. "We haven't had any fun in months."

"Okay, okay," I said. "We'll go to the beach."

I put the dinghy in the water and mounted the outboard. It fired right up but stalled on the way in. When I pulled the starter rope, it broke off in my hand. We were dead in the water, drifting towards some rocks. I quickly deployed the oars and started rowing.

"We're going back to the boat," I said. "I can't fix it on the beach."

I knew she was disappointed but I'd had enough for one day. I got to sit and drink my beer after all.

The next morning I set to work repairing the outboard. I brought it back aboard so I wouldn't lose any parts in the water. I had to remove the gas tank to get to the rewind mechanism. When I pulled that off, springs shot out and scattered across the deck. The main spring had come uncoiled and was twice its normal size. Every time I tried to rewind it, I lost my grip and it sprung out again. I started sweating and cussing. It took me over an hour to finally get the thing back together. I put it back on the dinghy and pulled. It wasn't right. More cussing commenced. I pulled it back off and repeated the process, taking care not to lose that spring again. When I was finished the second time, I had one tiny spring left over. I pulled the rope out and let it rewind a few times. It felt normal. I guessed I didn't really need that little spring. The motor fired up and we finally headed to the beach.

We spent an hour looking for shells and wading along the shoreline. We found a trail heading up a steep hill and took it. It led to a blue hole in the interior of the island. It was an amazing site to see. We heard voices coming up the hill from another trail. We froze for a second before realizing it couldn't possibly be anyone looking for us. It turned out to be a group of teenagers that had brought a fast boat from Nassau to see the blue hole. We watched as they took turns jumping off a steep cliff into the water below. They asked us to take a picture of their group. Brody obliged. They were the only people we saw that day. Hoffman's was a good place to be.

Over the next few weeks, we explored the area in our dinghy. We found Robinson Crusoe beach. We discovered the pure white sand at White Cay. The shelling was great at Devil's Cay. Brody posed with a giant red starfish that we found in the shallow bay just north of our anchorage. During that time, we noticed a few boats come and go from a rolly anchorage at White Cay. These were deep draft sailboats that couldn't make it through the shallow draft route that we had taken. We kept our anchorage to ourselves.

Through great conservation, we managed to make our water supply last for a month. It was time to go find more. We hated to leave, but we had to fill our tanks. We cruised down to Chub Cay and pulled up to the fuel dock. They charged us forty cents per gallon to take on water, and three dollars per bag to take our trash. I didn't want to take a slip in the marina, for fear that somehow we'd be found as a result. We anchored outside. We took the dinghy back in later to see what we could see. There was no TV anywhere or any political talk on the docks. We learned nothing except where the fish had been biting that day.

We went back north to a place called Bonds Cay. We anchored alone off a rocky shoreline. We found a nice beach near there too, and also had it to ourselves. We went back to Hoffman's and spent another three weeks soaking up the sun. Eventually, we grew anxious for news. We were also running out of beer.

"Can we make a run to Nassau?" asked Brody.

"Before entering the harbor, all boats must check in with the harbormaster," I told her. "They'll ask for the vessel's name and documentation number."

"I guess we'll just have to go without beer," she said.

"Let's not get hasty," I said. "Let me look at the charts."

I showed Brody a place called West Bay, on New Providence Island. It was a few miles from the center of Nassau. I knew it to be a good anchorage from a previous trip. I'd limped in there on my way to the Exumas to rendezvous with Holly and a boatload of hippies.

"That's pretty far to carry cases of beer," she said.

"We'll have to call a cab," I said.

"We don't have a phone," she said. "Remember?"

"So we walk to town, then find a cab on the street somewhere," I suggested.

"Can we spend some time in Nassau?" she asked. "I know you hate being around people, but I could use some interaction."

"I think we'll be adequately anonymous there," I said. "Maybe we can find a library with internet, or at least a bar playing CNN or Fox News."

"Point us towards New Providence, captain," she said.

"Land of pirates and millionaires," I said.

"We should fit right in."

It was an easy trip. *Leap of Faith* was running nicely and we encountered no problems. We anchored along a shoreline covered with upscale homes. It was too late in the day to make the trek to Nassau, so we settled on the back deck to await the sunset.

"We're going to have to make a move sooner or later," I said.

"What kind of move?" she asked. "What are you referring too?"

"This whole FBI mess," I said. "This living seems pretty easy, but remember what happened the last time we stayed gone for a long time."

"We both got antsy to return to Florida," she said.

"If we decide to stay on the run," I said. "We'll have to be committed to it long term."

"I see what you mean," she said. "Sooner or later we're going to need to use our passports. We'll need a critical part or we'll get questioned by Immigration or some other agency."

"Sooner or later," I said. "Unless we joined some expat community someplace. Ditch the boat and hide in the jungles of Ecuador or some such."

"That doesn't sound too appealing," she said. "But I simply don't know how to get out of this mess."

"I'm just thinking out loud here," I said. "Not suggesting anything, but what if we faced it head-on?"

"How so?"

"Get to the right people," I said. "Blow the whistle on the whole thing. Get the truth out there."

"That's a pretty big deal, Breeze," she said. "I'd be at the center of everything. Right now nobody knows my name outside the Bureau. I'm not sure I want to face that."

"Just thinking it through," I said. "Sometimes the toughest thing to do is the right thing to do."

"Have you always lived your life by that maxim?" she asked.

"Oh hell no," I said. "Mostly I just run. Try to avoid the responsibility, kind of like we're doing now."

"That seems a reasonable course of action in this situation," she said. "That's why we're here."

"I don't disagree," I said. "But let's take it a step further. Who would you contact with your story?"

"There are two sides to this battle," she began. "The Deep State boys want to take down Trump. That's what this is all about. Has been from the beginning. So Trump's inner circle would be the place to go. They'd have a sympathetic ear at least."

"Can't exactly call the White House and ask for a meeting with The Donald," I said. "Do you know anyone with any connection to his administration?"

"Never traveled in those circles," she said. "I doubt I even know anyone who might know someone."

"Can we send out a few emails?" I asked. "See who bites?"

"If I start sending emails to members of Congress, the FBI will be on us within hours," she said. "They'd probably be on us if I sent an email to my mom."

"Even from one of those library computers?"

"It's not the computer they need," she said. "It's the email account. They've already got that. I'm sure it's monitored."

"I know this isn't my area of expertise," I said. "But open up a new one, anonymously."

"You may find this hard to believe," she said. "But they read every email that a lawmaker opens or sends. Especially anyone they consider the opposition. Anyone in Washington that could help me is under electronic surveillance."

"They have the manpower for that?"

"The NSA does," she said. "It's not just manpower. It's computer power. It's complicated."

"Infernal machines will be the death of us all," I said. "George Orwell and whatnot."

"As backward as I think you are sometimes," she said. "I'm afraid you're right about this. You could never have eluded the FBI if you had a phone and a computer."

"Score one for backward Breeze," I said.

"Which gets us no closer to a solution," she replied.

"Still thinking," I said. "What we need is someone with the political gravitas to speak on your behalf to someone who can help. Someone in power. Keep you protected in exchange for your testimony."

"Testimony?" she said. "You think I'm going to testify against the FBI? You think I'm going to go up against Mueller and Comey and the rest of them? That's insane."

"Why is it so crazy?" I asked.

"Look, I'm just little old Brody, a former field agent," she said. "There are plenty of powerful people in Washington who know the same things I know. Let them iron it all out."

"Do you see any of them doing anything about it?" I asked. "Bunch of hot air and horseshit it looks like to me."

"Maybe Director Wray will do the right thing," she said. "If he's in there to straighten out the problems within the FBI, he can't let this Mueller investigation continue. He's got to stand up for what's right."

"And you say this about the guy who you think could have you killed?"

"Wishful thinking maybe," she said. "Just looking at both sides of the fence."

"Do you really think that an attempt on your life is a real possibility?" I asked.

"I don't know, Breeze," she said. "Stranger things have happened."

"I don't even want to know about it," I said. "Less I know the better."

I got up and walked to the fridge. I returned with two beers. The current political scene in America was a maze of bullshit I'd never be able to navigate. I was happy to be a boat bum, far removed from it all. Brody had brought wondrous things into my life, but she'd also brought this. I couldn't fix it. I could carry her across the seven seas if that's what she chose to do, but I could not do anything about what was going on in Washington. She could though. If she were strong enough, she could change the course of things back there. She could be the one to make a difference. On the other hand, if she opted to stay on the run, I was good with that. It's what I did best.

Ten

The walk into Nassau was longer than I expected. There was no direct route, and no one was picking up hitchhikers. We stopped at the first café we found for a cold drink. Every single tourist was either looking at their phone or using it to take pictures. The guy behind the bar was poking a finger at his phone between pouring drinks. I felt like an alien in a world of perpetually connected zombies.

Brody wanted to find the library. Her requests for directions were met with curious looks. Who goes to a library when on vacation in the Bahamas? What kind of weirdo was she? We finally got directions. It was on the other side of town and not in the best neighborhood, we were told. We stopped at a few more shops and bars as we slowly made our way across town. I was surprised to notice security cameras on the street. The closer we got to the port, the more of them I saw. It was probably a reaction to increased crime. It was a little spooky to think we were being watched.

We stumbled upon an internet café. It advertised free Wi-Fi, but we had no device. Brody dragged me inside to see if she could rent computer time from them. There were a half-dozen television sets mounted on one wall. One of them was tuned to C-Span.

"There he is," she said, pointing at a TV.

"Who?"

"Director Wray," she said. "Right there."

She turned to the girl behind the counter.

"Can you turn that one up, please," she asked.

"Who cares about them politicians," the girl said.

"Please, it's very important," said Brody.

The girl grudgingly turned up the volume.

When each man spoke, the TV pointed out his name and position. I knew none of the players, but it appeared that the FBI Director, Christopher Wray, was being grilled by members of Congress. This was a House Judiciary Committee appearance. The first few speakers used their time to blow smoke up our asses, but Representative Jim Jordon from Ohio got more to the point. He asked Wray if Peter Strzok was involved in writing up the application for a FISA warrant to surveil members of Trump's team. That got my attention. He then asked if the now-infamous fake dossier was used to convince the FISA court to give its approval. A hush fell over the proceedings. The camera zoomed in on Wray. He said that he could not legally release that information and that an inspector general was looking into the matter. Jordon was incredulous. He told Wray that all he had to do was show the warrant application to Congress. Wray stonewalled him, saying he would not discuss anything to do with the FISA court in that setting. Jordon continued to push Wray, but he wouldn't budge. He wasn't going to answer the questions and that was that.

Brody and I looked at each other. She nodded to the clerk that she could turn down the volume.

"What's that tell you?" I asked her.

"It tells me he's not there to clean up the FBI at all," she answered. "He's continuing the cover-up."

"What's that mean for us?"

"I don't know," she said. "Nothing good."

"Sorry to hear that," I said. "I'm sorry your career turned out this way."

"Listen," she said. "There are a lot of good men and women in the FBI. They're out there every day doing a fine job. They take their oaths seriously. This is a top-down problem. Mueller, Comey, McCabe, and now Wray. They are too powerful for someone like me."

"Didn't you say that everyone at the Bureau knew what was going on?" I asked.

"Anyone who doesn't have their head up their ass," she said. "And I know what you're getting at. This is their lifelong dream, to be an FBI agent. It's their career. It's taking care of their families and leaving a legacy. It's something to be proud of. Okay, so there's disappointing stuff going on up top. They can't do anything about that. They just go about their jobs like true professionals. They won't risk everything they've worked for to get involved in this."

"I don't understand the level of power we're talking about here I guess," I said. "If so many people know, like that Jordon guy on TV, why isn't anything being done about it?"

"You remember Hoover?" she asked.

"Herbert or J. Edgar?" I asked. "Vaguely."

"J. Edgar ran the FBI like the Gestapo," she said. "He had secret files on everybody. He had dirt on anyone who was important or might someday become important. He wasn't afraid to use it. Nixon was even afraid of the guy."

"That's what Mueller and Comey are doing now?"

"They know that your kid is a drug addict," she said. "They know your daughter had an abortion. They know that you like to get a happy ending at the Asian massage parlor every now and then. They know your taste in hookers or booze or that you cheat on your wife."

"Sounds like blackmail to me," I said.

"It's very effective," she said. "Let me assure you. No one has an empty closet."

"So they control the politicians," I said.

"And judges," she said. "Even presidents."

"The Deep State is real," I said. "And we are on their radar."

"I'm probably not on their top ten list of things to do right now," she said. "Considering the climate in Washington, but yeah, our names are on somebody's desk."

"Let's get some beer and go back to the boat," I said. "We've seen enough for one day."

We managed to get four cases of beer back to the boat. The cabbie wasn't happy to leave the city limits of Nassau, but an extra twenty persuaded him. Forty-five dollars per case plus the cab ride made for some expensive beer. I was going to have to ration it at that price. The next day we went back and stocked up on rum. It was only eight dollars per bottle. After getting groceries, we had everything we needed, except blood pressure medication. I was running low. Brody assured me that my doctor wouldn't call in a prescription to a Nassau pharmacy.

"Can we see a doctor here?" I asked. "Find one that takes cash?"

"I can't exactly Google it," she said. "I'm pretty sure they have their own type of universal care, but it wouldn't apply to foreigners."

"Do I really need the pills?" I asked. "I feel fine."

"Maybe if you quit the booze you wouldn't need them," she said. "Otherwise we'll need to find a way to get them."

"It would be simple enough back in Florida," I said.

"Maybe it's safe to go back," she said. "But maybe it's not."

"Not knowing sucks," I said. "Which is why we need a resolution to our FBI problem."

"I just don't know what that would be," she said. "I can't just show up in Washington and start singing."

"What about the press?" I asked.

"Jesus, Breeze," she said. "You really have been living under a rock. The press would immediately leak my name. There would be zero confidentiality. They'd botch the story and we'd never have any privacy again. My name and face would be everywhere. That is if we survive the repercussions."

"I've got an idea," I said. "Someone important that I can talk to. Someone with real power and connections."

"Who?"

"Fred Ford," I said. "Captain Fred to me. We go way back. I might even be able to find him."

"The name sounds familiar," she said. "Who is he, exactly?"

"Formerly of Pan Am," I said. "Think Lockerbie. Before that, Dallas Airport and Boston Port Authority. Most recently that airport in sugar country, near Clewiston."

"I vaguely remember his testimony before Congress on the Lockerbie bombing," she said. "How well do you know him?"

"We go way back," I said. "I met him down in the Exumas. He was the self-proclaimed commodore of the Red Shanks Yacht and Tennis Club, though nary a tennis court could be found. We've been through some stuff together."

"Where would he be now," she asked. "Still in the Exumas?"

"He went back to Florida a while back to tidy up his airport deal," I said. "Made about a billion bucks. Last I knew, he split his time between the city of Fort Myers and Fort Myers Beach. He wasn't at the beach when we went through, so he's likely in the City Yacht Basin."

"He'll help us?" she asked. "How can you be certain? No point in going back there if he says no."

"He's always been willing to help in the past," I said. "But this is bigger. He's the only person in my universe that has the kind of connections we need. I've helped him as well, so I think he'd be willing."

"I'll have to trust your judgement," she said. "Is he that connected?"

"The most connected person I've ever met," I told her. "From politicians to mobsters. He knows the important people."

"And you're his friend?" she said. "No offense intended."

"It started out as a casual thing," I said. "He helped me with some boat stuff. But then I saved his daughter from some poor decisions. I also saved him from the clutches of an evil lawyer lady."

"So he owes you?" she asked.

"It's not just that," I said. "We really are friends, but yes. Let's say he will be inclined to offer whatever assistance he can."

"I guess we're going back to Florida then," she said.

"Looks like it," I said. "Best thing I can come up with."

"Wing it and pray," she said. "Breeze's secret to strategic planning."

"He'll come through for us," I said. "Then you'll have to come through. If he gets you in front of the right people, you'll have to be ready to talk."

"I reserve the right to back out at any time," she said. "If it doesn't feel right, I'm bailing."

"Fair enough," I said. "You've got your instincts too."

We set out towards Gun Cay before first light, but we couldn't make our destination before dark. Instead of continuing after sunset, I pulled a mile or so off our charted course and dropped the anchor on the Banks. It was an eerie feeling, sitting there out of sight of land with the anchor down. I drank two precious beers and turned in early.

We arrived at Gun at ten in the morning. We could see the ocean through the cut. It was flat calm. We needed eight hours to cross the Gulf Stream. We'd make it by six that evening if things went well. I decided to keep going. I set a course for Biscayne Bay and settled in for another long day of travel. We could barely tell where the water ended and the sky began. The sky was impossibly blue, reflecting off the glass-like surface of the ocean. It was a glorious day to be on a trawler. *Miss Leap* purred like a contented kitten all day long.

I woke from a nap to find us off course. The autopilot was still working, but the current had pushed us much further north than I'd calculated. When I adjusted course, we lost speed dramatically. Our ETA was now after dark. I had no desire to navigate the narrow entrance in the dark. I recalculated based on the stronger flow of the current. I couldn't continue to fight it. If we let it carry us north, we'd break free of it somewhere near Miami. That was close enough. We rolled with it, crab-walking west by northwest towards the south Florida coast.

When I felt the current subside, I angled back southwest until we made the markers for Biscayne Bay. We took the first cut past the stilt houses and along the shoreline of Key Biscayne. We entered No Name Harbor well before dark and dropped anchor in the soft mud. It felt good to be back in Florida, even though that might mean we were closer to trouble.

"Turn your spidey senses back on," I told Brody. "We are once again back under the nose of our domestic policing agencies."

"The trail we left is a convoluted one," she said. "No one can know where we are."

"We're in Florida," I said. "Land of Breeze and *Leap of Faith*."

"If I was calling the shots I'd have someone watching our marina," she said. "I'd have someone hanging around the dinghy dock in

Fort Myers Beach, and maybe someone in downtown Punta Gorda."

"What about Pelican Bay?" I asked.

"I'd work with a local agency to do a flyover every few days," she said. "Sheriff's department or FWC. Whoever was most willing to cooperate."

"What about the Keys?"

"They aren't as familiar with your travels as I am," she said. "But Boot Key would be the only place worth looking."

"Planes and choppers fly over the harbor every day," I said. "Any one of them could keep an eye out for us."

"So we avoid it," she said. "And all the other likely places."

I spread a chart of the area out on the salon table. It was deeply familiar to me, but I wanted Brody to follow along as I plotted our likely route.

"We'll be okay for one night on the inside of Islamorada," I said. "We'll get there late in the day. We won't be spotted after dark. We'll leave early and cross Florida Bay in the old Yacht Channel. Can't do it at night due to all the lobster traps."

"We're not stopping in Little Shark River are we?" she asked.

"From Cape Sable, we'll angle out into the Gulf," I said. "We'll get way out there, beyond the crab pots. We do an overnighter to Marco."

"Hide up in Smokehouse Bay for the night," she said.

"Yes, and get groceries if needed," I said. "The next day we run up the Caloosahatchee to Fort Myers Yacht Basin."

"We'll be exposed coming in past the beach," she said.

"San Carlos Bay is wide open but heavily trafficked," I said. "It will take an hour or so to get under the bridge at Punta Rassa. Anyone looking will have to be right there during that hour."

"The odds are in our favor," she said. "If there's anyone out there looking at all."

"We'll be fine up the river in Fort Myers," I said. "It's not a normal haunt of mine. Local law enforcement aircraft run up and down the beaches. They never stray too far from the coast."

"Who else might be on the lookout for this boat?" she asked.

"Coast Guard if called upon," I said. "I've been watching the air traffic for years. Even they stay near the coast unless on an emergency. Civil Air Patrol covers Charlotte Harbor and Pine Island Sound. Sheriffs are looking for poachers. FWC is looking for rules violators, drunks and such."

"We'll be a needle in a haystack," she said. "Going slow and staying sober. Just another boat on the waterway."

"Practically invisible," I said. "The problem will be after. If we don't find Captain Fred we've got no place to go."

"What's your call on that?" she asked. "How sure of this are you?"

"I'm not," I admitted. "He's a rich man and until recently he's been a world traveler. He could be anywhere on the planet, but it's the only lead I have."

"Are we putting ourselves in a corner?" she said. "What if it's a dead-end?"

"He'll have neighbors," I said. "Someone might know where he is or how to get in touch with him. Marina staff will have his number."

"You would have made a good field agent," she said. "You think like a spy."

"Obstacles are made to be overcome," I said. "There's generally a way around whatever problems present themselves."

"Let's just say that he's not there and no one talks," she said. "He must guard his privacy. Staff won't give out his personal information."

I scratched my chin and thought it through for a minute. How do I get his attention? How can I make him appear through the force of my will? I remembered his camera system.

"I'll simply board his boat," I said. "Wave to the camera. He'll get an alert and check it out. He'll see me standing there."

"That will bring him running?"

"I'd like to think so," I said.

"If not?"

"I don't know yet," I said. "I'm hoping he's there or shows up soon after we arrive."

"Hope is not a good strategy," she said.

"Oh ye of little faith," I said. "It's all I've got at the moment. If you come up with a better plan along the way, feel free to speak up."

Eleven

I appreciated the way we worked together. She was a trained operative. I had my powers of observation and lengthy experience staying underground. We made a good team. She didn't belittle the extreme measures I took to stay hidden. She understood what we were up against.

We left Key Biscayne early in the afternoon. We arrived at Islamorada just before dark. As soon as we had a glimmer of light the next morning, we set out across Florida Bay. Lobster traps dotted the surface by the thousands. It was not a good time of year to be a lobster. I couldn't see how any of them survived that gauntlet of traps. Avoiding them took concentration. The autopilot was useless. I zigged and zagged through the obstacle course until we reached the protected waters of

Everglades National Park, where there were no more traps.

I put us on a course that would take us far out to sea and engaged the autopilot. Brody took over with instructions to alert me when we reached depths of sixty feet or more. The stone crabbers wouldn't set their pots out that deep. We could run through the night without snagging one in our running gear. I tried to ease the tension in my neck and shoulders by lying down. Before I knew it, Brody was waking me up from a deep sleep. The night was dark.

"The boat sounds fine," she said. "It's time to turn to the north."

It took me a minute to fully regain consciousness. I checked our progress on the chart plotter. I checked our depth. The temperature and pressure gauges were within their normal ranges. I listened to the melodic throb of the diesel. All was well. I turned off the autopilot and turned us to the north. I steered for ten minutes until I was satisfied with our course, then re-engaged it. Our estimated time of arrival was before first light, so I slowed us down. I planned to arrive just as the sun came up. We'd be well hidden in Smokehouse Bay. Brody went below to get some rest.

I was alone with my thoughts. Even in the dark, the big wide ocean was a good place to think. I reflected on modern man's fear of silence. All of the gizmos and noise pollution prevented introspective thought. That's how most people seemed to prefer it. They were afraid to be alone with their own thoughts. I embraced it. The trick was, to be honest with myself. When I was alone I could admonish myself for mistakes without the judgement of others. I could learn from the day's events or plan my strategy for the days to come. I used that night to reconsider what we'd set out to do.

It was noble to think that Brody could come forward with information that should help set things straight in Washington. It was a cause that was bigger than ourselves, but it could change the course of our lives forever. We couldn't know what the unintended consequences would be. At first glance, we thought that the truth should win out. On second thought, would it really be the best thing for the country? Bringing down the FBI would send shock waves through every citizen that was paying attention. We'd lose faith in our justice system. We'd already lost faith in the politicians whose job it was to oversee them. If "Did Not

Vote" were a candidate, it would be president after the last election. Maybe folks didn't really care anymore. Was it worth the trouble to send Brody into the lion's den?

I attempted to consider further implications, but it was hard without more knowledge of the political process. I gathered that Trump had shaken things up with his ham-handed manner. The fact that he was an outsider must really piss off the Deep State. It appeared that they had worked feverishly to undermine his legitimacy since his election. I didn't really care about Trump, and I'd dropped off society's radar long ago. Why did I care about corruption within the FBI? Why should I care about any of it?

I cared about Brody. I cared about the fate of our country. That was the bottom line. As much as I hated to interact with society in general, this was still America. Men didn't fight and die so that some political hacks could execute a soft coup against a sitting president. We didn't win wars so that every citizen could be secretly surveilled by spooks in Washington. Law enforcement wasn't there to provide justice for one party only. Justice was supposed to be blind. My life had little purpose since dropping out. I'd been happy enough when none of it mattered. Now I had Brody. Her life mattered to me and to my sense of fairness. She'd committed no crime. She didn't deserve to be hounded by those assholes.

I realized my own role in this fiasco. Brody was still an agent in good standing when she began her pursuit of me. She could have gone back to that at any time. She chose to be with me instead. She'd made a powerful statement. She showed that her love for me was more important than her previous career. It was at least partially my fault that this was happening. I'd been wary of her at first. I could have sent her packing. Instead, I'd let her in. She won me over with that sparkle in her eyes. She proved herself by choosing me over her previous life.

I had to protect her. I had to figure out a way to keep her safe, even if that meant keeping her secrets.

I woke her before we reached Capri Pass into Marco. We anchored for the day and took stock of our provisions. We didn't need much, but we picked up a few items while it was convenient. Brody was anxious for news, but something told me not to hang out in public for long. I felt safer on the boat.

"Captain Fred will be up on the latest," I told her.

"If he's there," she said.

"Listen, Brody," I said. "If you want to turn and run right now, we can. If you don't feel right about this, then don't do it because I pressured you."

"We've come this far," she said. "I feel like I've started a chain of events that I need to see through."

"Okay," I said. "We'll talk to Fred. Let's see if the three of us can figure out the best way to keep you safe. Anything gets squirrely and we ditch the whole thing."

"Can you do that in good conscience?" she asked.

"If anything happened to you I would never be able to forgive myself," I said.

The next day we moved on. San Carlos Bay was only a five-hour trip. We came in behind a shrimp boat returning from the Gulf. As he entered Matanzas Pass we veered off for Punta Rassa. We were exposed for the next hour. We kept a lookout for planes, choppers and police boats. We made it under the bridge without being detected. The river narrowed as we continued north towards Fort Myers. It opened up some as we approached the Route 41 bridges.

I saw One-legged Beth's boat anchored near a spoil island in the center of the river. Several large yachts lined the outer docks of the yacht basin. I couldn't tell if Captain Fred's boat was there. We anchored up and lowered the dinghy. Before we could take off for the marina, I heard Beth yelling my name. She was standing on deck waving both arms. As anxious as I was to find Fred, I couldn't ignore her. We motored over to her boat.

"Breeze, Breeze, Breeze," she said. "I knew that was you."

"Good to see you, Beth," I said. "How are things with you?"

"Fine and dandy," she said. "This place is the best thing ever happened to me."

"Glad to hear it," I said. "I knew you'd get back on your feet."

"Back on my foot," she said, laughing. "I only got one."

She and Brody exchanged pleasantries after that.

"I got me a real job," said Beth. "Even with my disability, they're letting me make up to a certain amount."

"That's great," I said. "Gives you something to do."

"You'll never guess where," she said.

"Okay, where?"

"IHOP," she said. "Get it? A one-legged waitress, working at IHOP?"

The three of us laughed. It was good to see Beth smiling and happy. It was satisfying to know that I hadn't wasted my energy helping her out. I sensed that she could make it, she just needed a little kick in the ass to put her life together again.

I begged forgiveness for not hanging out longer, but we had important business to attend to. We took the dinghy in to look for Fred's boat, *Incognito*. We found it tied alongside a T-dock just inside the basin. After I shut the motor off, I could hear Fred's voice. He was on a business call. I tied off to his swim platform and waited for him to finish the call. When the voice stopped, I stood up and looked over the transom.

"I'm going to have to find a new marina," he said. "They'll let any old sea rat in this place."

"Permission to come aboard?" I asked. Brody stood beside me.

"As long as you've got a pretty woman with you," he said. "Otherwise I'm not so sure."

"Good to see you too, Fred," I said. "How's the lifestyles of the rich and famous?"

"Can't find enough to spend my money on," he said. "But I've taken a young bride who promises to help me with that."

"Congratulations," I said.

"Yet you manage to bring the beauties with barely any money at all," he said. "And you ain't exactly wildly handsome."

"I'll be an old coot like you soon enough," I said. "Let me enjoy it while I still can."

"Let me guess why you're here," he said. "What kind of trouble has found you this time?"

I introduced him to Brody and gave him the short version of our dilemma. Brody filled him in on more specifics.

"How's she do that?" asked Fred.

"Do what?" she said.

"Her eyes sparkle," he said. "It's quite charming."

"Careful," I said. "That's how she hooks you."

"I think I'm flattered," said Brody.

"You be careful too," I told her. "He might not look like much but he's got a way with the ladies."

"I've got money and a line of bullshit," he said. "I use both to my advantage."

We moved inside and Fred closed up his windows. He turned on some music to cover our voices. He hit a hidden button that was part of his security system.

"We can talk freely now," he explained. "I hold private meetings here that I don't want to be overheard."

"What do you think about our situation?" I asked.

"I think you're way in over your head, Breeze," he said. "But I think that most times you come around. I know that lawyer from Punta Gorda was out of your league, but you somehow managed to come out on top."

"She was a shrewd and cunning bitch," I said. "But nothing like the FBI."

"I've got no contacts within that leftist cabal of Clinton ass-kissers," he said. "I've got CIA contacts, and of course a bunch of politicians."

"But you understand what Brody's up against," I said.

"You've been out of touch," he said. "It's gotten worse."

"What happened now," asked Brody.

"You've heard of Bruce Ohr?" he asked.

"He's with the DOJ," she said.

"Associate attorney general," he said. "Pretty high up."

"How is he connected to this?" she asked.

"He's had multiple contacts with Christopher Steele," he said. "The spy who produced the fake dossier for Fusion GPS."

"That sounds fishy," I said.

"He also had a relationship with Glenn Simpson, the founder of Fusion GPS," he said. "He met with Steele just before the election, and with Simpson just after."

"Hillary's campaign paid Fusion for opposition research," said Brody. "They hired Steele."

"And it looks like Ohr took that phony document to the FBI," Fred said. "The Justice Department used it to obtain the FISA warrants to surveil Trump associates."

"It's proof that the DOJ worked with one candidate to influence the outcome of the election," said Brody.

"But it continued after Trump won," said Fred. "In an effort to delegitimize Trump's presidency."

"There's not much left that I know that hasn't already become public," she said.

"Maybe there's no need to spill anything," I said.

"Except I need the dogs called off," said Brody. "I can't live for the rest of my life wondering if the FBI is going to come after me."

"What is it that you're not telling me?" asked Fred.

"Hillary's server," she said. "Comey and Mueller know what was on it. They know that it's criminal. They know for an absolute fact that Hillary played fast and loose with information that was vital to national security. Classified information that was stolen by outside parties, probably Russia."

"A lengthy jail sentence for anyone not named Clinton," he said. "And what those in the know suspect, but can't prove."

"Information that I can't be allowed to reveal," she said.

"If you have proof, we can get that information to someone else," he said. "Once it becomes public, your knowledge of it means less."

"I only have my testimony," she said.

Fred paced around the salon of his Hatteras. He chewed an unlit cigar. He stopped pacing to ask Brody some questions. He resumed pacing, leaving a trail of tobacco in his wake.

"I have a very good friend that can likely help us," he said. "He'll know who to talk to."

"Who are we talking about?" I asked.

"Another Fred," he said. "Fred Smith, my FedEx buddy."

"You're friends with the founder of FedEx?" asked Brody.

"I told you he was connected," I said. "But how is the FedEx guy going to help?"

"He's a political animal," Fred said. "Runs in those circles. He owns a big chunk of the Redskins for crying out loud. He sponsored one of Joe Gibb's race cars. More importantly, he was offered the Secretary of Defense job by George W. Bush."

"No way," I said. "What were his qualifications for that post?"

"He's a Marine," he said. "I'd trust any Marine in that seat."

"What happened?" asked Brody.

"He turned it down," he said. "That's how we got Rumsfeld. When Rummy left, George came back and asked him a second time. He turned it down again."

"I can see where he'd be connected with the Washington crowd," I said.

"Hell, I knew him when he didn't have two nickels to rub together," Fred said. "He's worth a few billion now."

"Self-made man?" I asked.

"His daddy left him four million," he said. "He used it to form his upstart delivery company. Almost lost it all. Once, couldn't pay the fuel bill for his trucks. He took his last four thousand bucks to Vegas and turned it into twenty-eight thousand at the blackjack table. Covered his fuel for four more days, but it was enough to get him over the hump."

"Cool story," I said. "And he went from there to almost being our Secretary of Defense."

"I was fortunate enough to be in a position to help him out along the way," he said. "We've been pals ever since. He sunk some money into my airport scheme."

"Good friend to have," Brody said.

"If you'll excuse me," said Fred. "I'll go and ask him to be your friend too."

We retreated to the back deck, outside of Fred's secure bubble. Twenty minutes passed before Fred came out to join us.

"He's going to talk to some people," he said. "He promised to get in touch within a few days, after he's gotten a better handle on the situation."

"We'll need to hide in the meantime," I said. "We can't just sit here and wait for someone to find us."

"Take your boat up the river," he said. "I'll pick you up in my tender. You'll stay here with me."

"I can't put you out like that," I said.

"Nonsense," he said. "You'll be safe here. I take my security seriously."

He had a good point. He had plenty of space, the ability to communicate without anyone listening, and a sophisticated security system. It was the ideal place to law low for a few days. I also knew that Fred liked to cook gourmet meals for his guests. There was no reason to turn that down.

"Thanks, Fred," I said. "You're a good man."

"We appreciate your help and hospitality," said Brody.

"Think nothing of it, young lady," he said. "It is I who will be privileged by your presence."

"Give us a couple of hours," I said. "We'll get past the next set of bridges and look for a place to anchor."

"I'll pick you up in time to return before dark," he said.

We swung by Beth's boat but she wasn't home. I raised our anchor and motored us further up the river. We went under I-75 and through the old railroad bridge. I found a place to anchor well below the first lock. We packed a few things before Fred arrived. I left the dinghy trailing behind the boat. It would give the impression that someone was aboard. I freed a stack of hundred dollar bills from one of my hiding places and locked her up tight.

Fred showed up and we loaded our stuff into his tender. It was a fast ride back down the river to the yacht basin. He checked the control panel for his cameras. Nothing unusual had happened in his absence.

"I've got a beautiful rib roast that needs to be enjoyed," he said. "You two make yourselves comfortable. There's beer and wine in the back fridge. Help yourself to whatever you'd like."

I grabbed two beers out of the fridge. Fred fired up his grill. He offered me a fine cigar, which I accepted. He offered one to Brody too, but she declined.

"How did this happen?" asked Brody. "One minute I'm hiding in the swamp swatting mosquitoes, haven't showered in two weeks, running for my life. The next thing I know we're sitting in the lap of luxury, about to eat a fine meal on a fancy yacht."

"Just lucky, I guess," I said.

"No," she said. "You're the one who wanted to come here. You were sure we'd find him. I was skeptical about the whole thing. I just can't see how you two are friends, but clearly, you are."

"Not too many men like Breeze left in this world," said Fred. "I know he's a hard man, but he was there for me when I needed him. Never hesitated. That's the kind of people you want in your life. If you can endure his lifestyle, you'd do well to hold on to him."

"Endure is a good word, captain," she said. "But I'm afraid it's me that's brought trouble to his door this time."

"Appears he's doing everything in his power to help you out of this jam," he said. "He was right to come to me."

"Do you think your friend can help?" she asked.

"He'll see which way the wind is blowing in that festering cesspool," he said. "Figure out a way to assert himself without getting shit on his hands."

"We're a lot better off than we were," I said. "We've got some real influence on our side now."

"Not bad work for a boat bum," said Brody. "I'm still trying to figure out how you do it."

"He's got the knack," said Fred. "Probably should have been dead or drowned a long time ago."

"Long live Breeze," I said.

Twelve

FedEx Fred called two days later. He wanted to come to Incognito to meet Brody before he stuck his neck out on her behalf. It seemed like a reasonable request. He arrived in a black SUV. He was not driving. His driver was clearly a bodyguard. He and Captain Fred exchanged insults before introductions were made. FedEx Fred looked to be in his early seventies. He had white hair that had receded slightly. He was a little soft in the middle and had more flesh around the neck and chin than he needed, but his eyes were sharp. He gave me a long look, sizing me up, before turning his attention to Brody. I hoped that Captain Fred had assured him that I was good people.

The driver stationed himself at the back door. The rest of us went inside for some privacy. Brody turned on the sparkle once she was face to face with FedEx Fred, but he was all business.

"There have been further developments since Fred first called me," he said. "As usual, the press had omitted some key details."

"What now?" asked Brody.

"This Bruce Ohr from Justice," he said. "His wife actually worked for Fusion GPS."

"How can that little tidbit have escaped scrutiny?" asked Captain Fred.

"Mueller only demoted Ohr after this was discovered," said FedEx Fred. "In the meantime, she was using a HAM radio to keep her communications secret."

"Old school," I said. "Spooks can't be listening to HAM radio, can they?"

"Doubtful," said FedEx Fred. "But it's clear that Mueller's investigation is horribly compromised."

"Where is Director Wray in all of this?" asked Brody. "He seems to be awfully quiet."

"He's quite busy attempting to protect the FBI's secrets," he said. "You are only one of a thousand loose ends, and a small one at that."

"Is that good news?" she asked.

"Is there anyone actively searching for us?" I added.

"It is my understanding that there is no current pursuit," he said. "But all the usual alerts remain. You've managed to avoid those so far."

"We don't want to have to continue avoiding them indefinitely," said Brody.

"Your file is near the bottom of a large stack," he said. "No one is reviewing whether or not finding you is still necessary. Wray is getting heat from all sides. His hands are full covering his ass."

"And Comey's," said Captain Fred. "And Mueller's."

"How do we get his attention," asked Brody. "Can we get him to simply close that file and turn off the alerts?"

"You're still a threat to him," said FedEx Fred.

"Great," I said. "Where do we go from here?"

"I'd like to take Brody to Washington," he said. "Get her in front of the right people. Bring her out of the shadows so that those in power can see her as a real person. Impress enough of them so that they'll get the message to Wray not to mess with her, but not in any official proceeding."

"Closed door meetings?" I asked. "No testimony at any hearing?"

"That's my advice," he said. "You don't won't to blow the lid off this thing. It won't come with good consequences for you."

"All we want is to be left alone," I said. "That's all we've ever wanted."

"I can have a jet at Page Field this afternoon," he said. "I'll have my people make accommodations for all of us. I'll get you in front of the players. It's your game after that."

"Do it," said Captain Fred. "He knows what he's doing. Trust him."

"It's worth a try," said Brody.

"I'm with her," I said. "Let's do it."

We were dismissed. We went out back to let the two Freds talk in private. I tried to make small talk with the bodyguard. He didn't have much to say. He obviously took his job seriously. Eventually, he would drive us to a small airport in Lee County. We all boarded a corporate jet and took off for D. C.

We were put up in a fine hotel and told to order room service. Both Fred's worked their contacts and arranged meetings for the next two days. Brody was relieved that she wouldn't be appearing before some congressional committee, but nervous about whomever she was about to meet. I was informed that I wasn't invited to these meetings by Captain Fred. I understood completely. I'd be of no help to her, other than moral support. I'd have to give that from the hotel room.

FedEx Fred laid out the itinerary. Her first stop was the White House. She'd be speaking with General Kelly, the White House Chief of Staff.

"Won't my name be on the visitor's log?" she asked.

"We want them to know," he said. "Word will get out quickly."

Her next meeting would be with Trey Gowdy at the Capital Building. Both Freds would accompany her, making a show of their entrance. Gowdy would introduce the trio to various lawmakers as they were available. Sympathy for her cause would be drummed up. Campaign donations would be dangled. The combined financial and political wherewithal of the two Freds would be brought to bear. FBI Director Christopher Wray would soon find the need to lose Brody's file, and forget she ever existed. That was the plan anyway.

I marveled at what I'd wrought from the hotel bar. An anonymous boat bum had stormed Washington with a small army of influential people, not to bring about real change, but to keep his woman safe. We'd lost our original mission somewhere along the way, but we had come to terms with it. We had no business thinking we could impact the political landscape, and little desire. Still, it was a lot to grasp. Captain Fred was my friend. He'd helped me out before, but nothing like this. I must have really meant something to him. Sure, I'd helped him too, but now I was going to be forever in his debt. I'd be quick to repay him if and when the time came.

When they returned Brody looked worn out. I gave her a hug and thanked the Freds profusely.

"I'll be getting some feedback before the end of the day tomorrow," said FedEx Fred. "Then I need to fly out."

They left Brody and me alone for the night.

"How was the White House visit?" I asked.

"Kelly was gracious and kind," she said. "He took me seriously."

"Did you see Trump?" I asked.

"No, but I asked if the President would know about my visit," she replied. "He said that it was his job to inform the President of such matters."

"Did he give you any indication of how he felt about the FBI and the DOJ?" I asked. "There has to be some friction there."

"He did not," she said. "He was nothing but professional."

"What about Gowdy and the rest of them?"

"They seemed to appreciate getting information that they could pressure Wray with," she said.

"You told them about the server?"

"I had no choice," she said. "I needed to give them something in order to get something in return."

"Quid pro quo," I said.

"This place runs on it," she said. "Scratch my back is how it works."

"By tomorrow the word will be out," I said. "Agent Brody meets with all the important opposition and spills her guts. That's supposed to make them leave you alone."

"Or what I said will be used against them," she said. "It's a threat."

"Will it work?"

"Time will tell," she said. "We gave it a hell of a shot. Thanks for all of this, Breeze."

"Thank me after we get the all clear," I said. "I don't trust any of them, on either side."

The next evening Brody and I huddled with the two Freds to hear what they'd learned.

"Did we accomplish anything?" asked Brody.

"The outcome is positive," said FedEx Fred. "But not in the way that we planned."

"We also learned that the sordid web of corruption is even more tangled than we could have imagined," said Captain Fred.

"What now?" Brody asked.

"Andrew McCabe," said FedEx Fred.

"The second in command at the FBI," said Brody.

"You may remember his wife running for a Senate seat in Virginia," he said. "McCabe was about to drop an investigation bomb on Virginia's governor."

"Terry McCauliffe."

"Right," he said. "McCauliffe comes up with seven hundred thousand dollars to donate to her campaign."

"Assistant director is about to investigate a governor," she said. "Assistant director's wife is running for office. Governor under suspicion donates a huge amount to her campaign."

"You can guess what happened next," he said.

"Investigation goes nowhere," she said.

"Precisely," he said. "Now McCabe has an Ohr and Strzok problem. He was supposed to testify before the House Intelligence Committee, but has suddenly developed a scheduling problem."

"Is there anyone in this town that isn't a corrupt scumbag?" I asked.

"It gets worse," said Captain Fred. "But it's inconsequential to why we came here."

"Where do I stand in all of this?" asked Brody.

That was the crux of the matter. We'd invested these two men's time and money to earn Brody her freedom. The amount of influence we'd been able to exert was more than we could have hoped for. Was it enough?

"Director Wray will forget that Brody ever existed," said FedEx Fred. "Brody will go about her business without fear of FBI reprisal."

"And keep my mouth shut," said Brody.

"Doesn't matter now," he said. "Certain members of the group we spoke to yesterday have already acquired the information from other sources. Now that Wray knows that, there is no reason for him to persecute you. The information is still out there."

"So when do the heads start rolling?" I asked.

"I don't believe they ever will," he said.

"The shit in the cesspool is thicker and deeper than we thought," said Captain Fred.

"There won't be any consequences for all this?" asked Brody.

"Listen," said FedEx Fred. "No one was ever going to indict Hillary Clinton, no matter how much hard evidence was presented. It's just never going to happen. All of the parties involved are doing what's been asked of them, therefore nothing will happen to them either. Trump was out there yesterday expressing his confidence in Director Wray, contrary to logical thought."

"What about Mueller's investigation into Trump?" I asked.

"Political theater," he said.

"Tell that to General Flynn," Brody said.

"Flynn's punishment will amount to nothing," he said. "And it won't hurt Trump. He's paying for his perceived aggressions against Obama's Deep State, not for anything to do with Russia."

I was losing track of the Byzantine plot. The cast of characters was large and the actions they'd taken were complicated. It made me sick to my stomach. I desperately wanted to go back to my boat and put it all behind me. There was more incentive than ever to stay off the grid. At least, Brody had her get out of jail free card. We could relax and enjoy life again.

"There's nothing we can do about the state of affairs in this town," said Captain Fred. "But at least we got what we came for. Brody is a free woman, my friend."

"I can't thank you two enough," Brody said. "Seriously, from the bottom of my heart."

"Me too, Freds," I said. "I'm touched that you'd go so far out of your way for us."

"The captain told me what you did for him," said FedEx Fred. "He needed a friend like you and you came through for him."

"I owed him," I said. "Still do. You too."

"If I ever need a character like you, I'll call in the favor," he said. "But for now, go home and enjoy your freedom."

"On that note," said Captain Fred. "I've got a phone for you. It has no GPS nor Wi-Fi capability. It can only make calls. Not traceable."

"Thanks, I guess," I said. "But we really have no use for it."

"I do," he said. "It has both of our numbers already programmed in. Keep it charged and answer when it rings."

"The Two Freds Bat Phone," I said. "Any-time you need me, I'll be there."

"I may just want you to bring this lovely young lady for drinks," he said. "Keep in touch this time."

"Thank you both," I said.

We flew back to Page Field outside of Fort Myers the next morning. Captain Fred had a car waiting to take us all back to the marina. It had been a heady trip. We'd flown with the bigwigs on their dime. Brody had met the powers that be. A message had been delivered on our behalf. The halls of justice needed a serious cleaning, but we'd gained our freedom. Let the bad apples rot, as long as it didn't interfere with our lives.

Thirteen

After promising Captain Fred that we'd stay in touch, we returned to *Leap of Faith*. She looked forlorn. She was always sad when I left her alone. Mildew had already started to form on the cabin ceiling. The interior smelled musty. We opened her up to let some fresh air inside.

"She's going to need a good scrubbing," said Brody.

"I noticed some of the teak needs touching up too," I said.

"Are we going to play or work?" she asked.

"Let's spend a few days in Pelican Bay," I said. "Unwind a little."

"Then can we go back to the marina?" she asked. "Please?"

"Sure," I said. "I can give Captain Lee a proper thank you."

"And I can take long hot showers," she said.

We motored to Pelican Bay under a cloudless sky. Dolphins played in our bow wake as we approached Cabbage Key. Things couldn't have been better, but something was nagging me. I couldn't shake the feeling that things weren't as right and proper as they seemed. On the surface, our efforts had paid off and the results were perfect. My sixth sense said otherwise, but wouldn't give me anything specific to focus on.

"We're good, right?" I asked Brody. "We can go back to being carefree and being in love?"

"Never loved you more," she said. "Why? What's up?"

"Something is telling me not to let my guard down," I explained. "I don't know why."

"I've learned not to ignore your hunches," she said. "What do you want to do?"

"I don't know," I said. "Just stay alert. Be tuned into anything out of the ordinary."

"Life with Breeze," she said.

"Life with Brody," I shot back.

"We're a hell of a pair," she said. "But at least we've got each other."

We spent a few days at anchor in Pelican Bay. We walked the beach and swam in the surf. I managed to catch a slot-sized snook for dinner one night. We watched the sun go down with drinks in hand. We made love each night, rocking gently along with the waves. No dark men lurked in the shadows. I spotted no binoculars spying on us from the other boats. No one followed us across the island to the beach. Maybe I'd been paranoid for too long, imagining threats that didn't exist.

I reluctantly agreed to head back to the marina. We needed to take care of *Miss Leap*. I needed to provide comfort for Brody. We'd made friends there. It was a nice place to be. The only drawbacks were being connected to land and being too close to society. My eyes shifted back and forth as we tied up in the slip. I looked for strange boats and strange people. I found none. A small greeting party showed up to welcome us back.

Captain Lee appeared and I shook his hand.

"I owe you, buddy," I said. "You really came through for us."

"It was fun," he said. "A little excitement for a change. Have you resolved whatever problems you had?"

"Long story, but yes," I told him. "We are trouble-free."

"Excellent," he said. "Enjoy your stay."

That's how it went for the next few days. People were genuinely happy to see us. They were friendly and helpful. The goodwill we felt was the polar opposite of the vibe in Washington. Brody scrubbed the walls and ceilings with white vinegar. The windows got washed. I sucked excess water out of the bilge to improve the atmosphere. Our little window unit air conditioner went back in the side door. Once Brody was happy with the interior, she started spending afternoons at the pool, rejuvenating her tan.

I went to work on the teak. I stripped and sanded the parts that needed it and refinished them with varnish. I caulked up leaky seams and window frames. I replaced old bilge pumps, even though they were still working. I tightened hose clamps and changed the oil and filters. We walked to the end of the dock each night for sunset social gatherings. We took a dip in the hot tub after dark.

Throughout it all, I kept my eyes and ears open. I made myself familiar with my surroundings. I learned who drove which car. I learned which boats had full-time liveaboards and which didn't. I watched the occupants of the condos on the property. I took note of the landscapers and pest control guys. I learned to recognize members of the staff from forklift drivers to dockhands. Brody carried her pistol wherever she went. I took her to the range to stay sharp with it. I cleaned up my old shotgun and kept it within easy reach. There was no sign of anything or anyone suspicious. Life went on.

Now that we were living in a peaceful, normal environment, I decided to call Daniel. We had the bat phone. Brody had written down his number. We both wanted to know how he was doing. He answered the strange number on the first ring.

"Where are you?" he asked. "Is everything okay?"

"We're fine," I told him. "We're back at the marina."

"Awesome," he said. "I want to come visit. I need to check on my boat too."

"Come on down," I said. "Brody would love to see you."

"We can go harass some sharks again," he said.

"Sure," I said. "Let us know when you're coming. We can pick you up at the airport."

The bat phone rang two days later. It was neither of the Freds. It was Daniel. He was flying in soon. Now we had three contacts in our clunky little flip phone. We drove to Fort Myers to pick him up. The airport creeped me out. There were too many people to watch. The place was clean and bright, but if someone wanted to do us harm, there wasn't much we could do about it. I hustled Daniel out to the parking garage.

"You act like someone's chasing us," he said.

"You never know," I said.

"Breeze is just being cautious," said Brody. "Probably over cautious."

On the way back we stopped at a nearby boatyard to check on Daniel's boat, *Lion's Den*. It was filthy. I gave Daniel a look of disapproval.

"I know, I know," he said. "I was in a hurry when I left. I'll get it cleaned up and covered before I go back."

"You're not going to put her back in the water?" I asked.

"Not enough time," he said. "I've got to get back to Enduring Warrior soon enough."

"How's that going?" I asked.

"Great," he said. "It's my purpose in life. Troy is awesome. He's kind of taking over for you as far as teaching me stuff."

"Good to hear," I said. "I can't hold your hand forever."

"I know you can't," he said. "That's why I went up there. It was a good choice."

"I'm proud of you," I said.

"Thanks, man," he said. "Means a lot."

Back at the marina, Daniel was greeted with enthusiasm, especially from the ladies. Men shook his hand. Women gave him big hugs. Mo planted a wet kiss on his cheek.

"You're handsomer than ever," she said. "You certainly have a girlfriend up there."

"Yup," he said. "And she's Irish."

"A match made in heaven I'm sure," she said. "Lucky lass."

We spent just one day getting ready before taking Daniel out to Cayo Costa to chase big fish. We had our system figured out from our earlier adventures there. We hooked a monster within an hour. Daniel was the rod man. Brody untied the dinghy. I drove after the beast while Daniel regained line. Eventually, we settled in for a Nantucket sleigh ride through Pelican

Bay. The fish didn't act like a shark or a tarpon. It stayed down low and kept pounding Daniel's arms with violent head shakes. We caught up with it after thirty minutes, but could not raise it from the bottom. It just sat down there under the dinghy, refusing to move.

Daniel tried to raise it to no avail. He looked at me for advice.

"Hell, I don't know," I said. "If we try to drag it the line will break."

"It must be wrapped around some rocks or something," he said. "I can't budge it."

My curiosity got the best of me. I wanted to see what we'd hooked and fought for the last half-hour. I took off my shirt and kicked off my flip-flops.

"You going in after it? Asked Daniel. "That's nuts."

"I don't think it's a shark," I said. "I've got to see what it is."

I put on a mask and eased over the side. Daniel kept tension on the line. I took a few deep breathes and went under, following the line down to my target. It was indeed wrapped around something. The fish had circled a sunken log and snagged himself. I found him hovering in place, wondering what the hell happened. It was a goliath grouper big enough to eat a man if he wanted to.

I went back up for air.

"What is it?" asked Daniel.

"Big ass grouper," I said. "He's hung up pretty good."

"We can't keep him," he said. "You want to cut him loose?"

"Don't you want to see him?" I asked. "He's huge."

"What about the rod?" he asked.

"He can't go anywhere until we free him," I said. "I think I can get the hook out if he lets me."

"You're certifiable," he said. "I'm not sticking my hand in some monster's mouth."

"He'd spit you out at the first taste," I said. "Give me some pliers. I'm going to try it."

"Hold on," he said. "I'm coming too."

We both went back down. I got to the fish's mouth and saw that he had several hooks in him. I pointed to them and waved Daniel over. The old rusty hooks came out easily. The big fish didn't fuss about it. He kept one big eye on me as I worked. He knew what I was doing. Daniel held him by the lower lip with gloved hands. I was running out of time. I needed some air. I motioned upward. Dan motioned downward and shook his head. I handed him the pliers and moved up to the surface.

A few seconds later the big fish was at my side. Daniel came up with him. The grouper hung there for a few seconds, as if to say thanks, then swam slowly away. Daniel and I exchanged high-fives. He got in the dinghy first and gave me a hand getting in. There was a time when I could have stayed down longer than him. Coming up early was another sign of my advancing age. I didn't like it.

Back on *Leap of Faith*, we found the last fifteen feet of line badly frayed. Daniel was ready to re-rig, but I'd had enough. It wasn't every day you came face to face with a six-hundred-pound fish. We couldn't top that. I decided that sitting in the sun and drinking beer was a better idea. After just one beer, Daniel started casting lures off the big boat. His energy supply was unlimited. He was always doing something. I'd been like that at his age. Decades of work and responsibility had beaten that out of me. I'd learned to relax. I no longer needed to be busy all the time. I actually enjoyed sitting around doing nothing. It was a luxury that most people couldn't afford.

Back in the real world, folks were taking their kids to soccer practice, mowing the lawn, paying the bills, doing the laundry and trying to figure out how to accomplish everything that needed to be done with the limited time they had. I sat on my boat in a peaceful cove, watching the birds fly by. I also watched the comings and goings of other boats. Even though I was relaxing, I was still aware of my surroundings. I stayed aware even when I had no reason to be. It was a rare event that took me by surprise.

I saw nothing to be worried about. Daniel was catching small trout. Brody was on the bridge reading a book. I drank my beer. I hoped that my intuition was wrong. I wanted to believe that there was no evil lurking out there, waiting to do us harm, but the feeling wouldn't go away. I told myself to be content, but something else bugged me. Those men and women in Washington would never be brought to justice. They played their espionage games and couldn't care less about what was best for the average citizen. They politicized everything and then wondered why the country was so divided. They consistently ignored the will of the people. They did not represent us. Our votes meant nothing to them. I believe it was Mark Twain who said "If our votes meant anything, they wouldn't let us do it."

I'd brushed against the rot that had taken hold of our institutions, and now I was infected. There was a bug in my ear, telling me that something bad was going to happen. I wondered if I was sensing that the country itself was in trouble, rather than Brody and me. I'd never given it much thought before. What I didn't know couldn't hurt me. Ignorance is bliss. My unwanted education into what was really going on didn't sit well with me. Maybe that's what was bothering me.

I considered leaving the country again. We were free to use our passports. We could go anywhere we wanted. I broached the subject with Brody but she was against it. The third-world didn't hold any charm for her. She enjoyed the comforts and convenience of living in America. I couldn't blame her. I'd grown accustomed somewhat to the marina life myself. She went as far as to suggest that we look into a bigger and newer boat.

I was stunned at first, but she had a list of good points. *Miss Leap* was old and required constant upkeep. Our sleeping quarters were cramped. We could use more storage. Our shower was a pain in the ass to use, even when we had unlimited water at the marina. The bridge needed a new enclosure. The teak maintenance never ended. The list went on and on.

"I would never demand that you sell her," she said. "I know how you feel about her. Just think about it, okay?"

"As long as this isn't some choice between you and her," I said. "Don't do that."

"I know," she said. "I just think we'd both be more comfortable with something bigger and newer. We can afford it for God's sake."

"It would have to be one hell of a perfect boat for me to even think about it," I said. "I guess I'd consider it if the right boat came along."

"I'll see what's out there," she said. "When we get back."

We spent a few more days enjoying the salt and the sun. Daniel had to get back up north, so we returned to the marina. Brody wanted to buy a new tablet to access the internet. The marina had a good Wi-Fi signal, but it only worked with newer devices. She came back from Best Buy with a new iPad. The first thing she did was shop for boats. After a thorough search, she handed me the device. She had saved several boats for me to look at. I didn't like any of them, except the one in South Carolina.

"This one is nice," I said. "But South Carolina is a haul."

"You didn't like any of the boats in Florida?" she asked.

"They've got no soul," I said. "All a bunch of marina queens."

"We live in a marina now," she pointed out. "That's what people do."

"I could rent a car and drive back," said Daniel. "Check it out for you on the way."

That gave me an idea. I didn't like Daniel's boat sitting there on the hard unattended. He didn't have time to take it back north. It was a long trip in a slow boat.

"What if we took *Lion's Den* up to you?" I asked. "We stop and check this boat out. Bring your boat on up to you."

"You'd do that?" he asked. "It's a hell of a long way."

"I've made the trip up to the Chesapeake once," I told him. "Seems like a good solution for you."

"I'll have to find a place to keep it," he said.

"It will take us a couple months," I said. "That's plenty of time."

"I'm good with it if you are," he said. "I'd be grateful."

"Pay it forward when you get the chance," I said. "You okay with this, Brody?"

"You hit me out of the blue," she said. "I wasn't expecting this."

"To be truthful," I said. "I've still got that feeling that something's not right. If we get out of here for a few months, maybe it will pass."

"They could have found us here easy enough," she said. "What makes you think someone would show up now?"

"Nothing specific," I said. "Maybe I'm a raving lunatic. I'd just feel better if we made ourselves scarce again, at least for a little while."

"We're not going to be on the run forever," she said. "There's no reason."

"We'll do this," I said. "Look at that boat. Find another one if it doesn't please us. Come back here and live happily ever after."

"Promise?" she said.

"I promise," I said. "If we find a boat that meets my expectations."

"All right," she said. "I'll go along."

"It will be fun," I said. "We'll take our time. See the sights."

I made arrangements to launch Daniel's boat later that week. We took him to the airport. It was easier saying goodbye when we knew we'd see him again soon. Both of us liked having him around.

The boatyard put *Lion's Den* on a dock to allow me time to check things over before departing. She was still in good shape and ready to go. Brody and I brought her the thirty-six miles around to the marina. It was a good shakedown cruise. The little sailboat handled well in a moderate breeze. We sailed her from the Myakka River to the ICW at Boca Grande, before motoring the rest of the way.

We took on provisions and moved some of our clothes onto *Lion's Den*. It felt quite cramped compared to *Leap of Faith*. Sitting down below gave me the feel of being in a submarine. Brody was not impressed either. She delayed our departure in order to clean the interior up a bit. Storage was limited so we kept our clothes in duffel bags. We'd be roughing it for the foreseeable future. Brody was angling for a bigger place to live. I'd put her into a smaller one. She was hoping for something more luxurious. Instead, we were camping in a minimalistic vessel. I was going to have to make it up to her.

Fourteen

Brody did her best to make the little boat comfortable, but she clearly wasn't thrilled with the accommodations. We also had a choice to make. Did we cut across the state via the Okeechobee Waterway, or did we swing down through the Keys to get to the east coast of Florida? *Lion's Den's* mast was fifty-one feet above the waterline. The lowest bridge we'd encounter on the cross-state route had a clearance of fifty-four feet. We'd save almost two hundred miles if we motored through the middle of the state. Sailing opportunities would be minimal.

"Any more downsides?" asked Brody.

"Bugs and locks," I said. "I don't like the locks much, but with you onboard, it will be easier."

"I don't like the bugs," she said. "What's the downside of going through the Keys?"

"It's longer, but we can sail more," I said. "If we don't put the sails up, there's no point in having that mast sticking up."

"We'll have to skip Little Shark," she said. "Speaking of bugs."

"That means an overnight sail from Marco," I explained.

"I'm no sailor, Breeze," she said. "I wouldn't be much good on a night watch under sail."

"It's a fifteen hour trip to Marathon," I said. "If we leave in the middle of the night, we can make it before sunset. Most of the trip would be after sunrise. I can take the first night shift and run until sunup."

"No bugs in the Gulf," she said. "I think I'd rather go down through the Keys."

"If we have any boat problems, we can fix whatever needs fixing in Marathon," I told her.

"Sounds like a plan," she said. "Make it so, captain."

We left the marina at the first hint of light. We traveled the ICW south until we reached the Boca Grande Pass. We went out into the Gulf on a perfect southwest Florida sailing day. The winds were out of the east at twelve knots. The sky was clear and the forecast was good.

We pushed Daniel's boat, tweaking the sails until we felt we were getting the most out of her. I imparted what little knowledge of sailing I had to Brody. I'd learned from Holly. She was a good teacher, but she had a feel for the wind and waves that I didn't have. She was one with her vessel and knew exactly how it would respond. We didn't have that luxury. I was happy to cruise along at six knots in benevolent seas. We made it to Marco just before sunset. The boat held up fine. I dropped the anchor in Factory Bay, planning a quick exit when we were ready to jump to Marathon.

After a quick bite, we both napped through the early evening. Brody checked the weather. Another good day was in store. We rose at two in the morning and prepared to leave.

"There isn't any wind," said Brody.

"It should pick up with the sunrise," I said. "We'll motor out."

She helped me get the anchor up and turn out to sea before going to bed. Under power, we only traveled at five knots. We needed to do better to get to Marathon before dark. I did my best to dodge crab traps as the boat sliced through the flat waters of the Gulf. The droning motor broke the silence.

Just before dawn, the first whiff of a breeze showed itself. I raised the jib and motor sailed. We picked up some speed. Brody brought coffee up as the sun rose over the mainland. By the time I'd finished my first cup, we had enough wind to shut down the engine. I raised the main and listened to the waves sluice along the hull. I tried to feel what *Lion's Den* wanted. I adjusted course and trimmed the sails, keeping an eye on our speed and general attitude.

We should have reached peak performance on a beam reach, but that's not what the boat wanted. She needed to be a few degrees off to the wind. This meant we'd eventually have to tack to maintain our course. Brody didn't quite understand. I tried to demonstrate.

"See how fast we're going right now?" I asked. "Feel the boat's preference for this angle."

"I don't feel anything," she admitted.

"Now watch when I bring her back to a true beam reach," I said.

We lost almost a full knot of speed. The boat seemed to argue with our approach.

"See?" I asked.

"We slowed down," she said. "But I still don't feel anything. I don't get it."

I let the boat fall off a few degrees. We picked up speed again. The strain on the rigging relaxed a bit.

"Feel that?" I asked.

"I think so," she said. "She seems happier this way."

"That's what I'm talking about," I said. "I'll make a sailor out of you yet."

"I don't think so," she said. "I'll stick to being a stink potter. Thank you very much."

"You and me both," I said. "But this does have a certain appeal. Like the sailing ships of old."

"Trust me," she said. "If those old sea captains could have installed a motor, every one of them would have."

"Probably so," I said. "But this is what we've got right now. Let's make the best of it."

We left a slight zig zag trail in our wake as we continued south. We sailed under the Seven Mile Bridge well before sunset. I left the sails up until we neared the channel entrance to Boot Key Harbor. I started the engine and Brody helped me bring them down. We motored into the mooring field. Most of the wreckage caused by Hurricane Irma had been cleared from the water, but there was still a mess on land. Some of the canals were piled up with debris and sunken boats. Many of the moored vessels showed obvious damage. Sailboats were de-masted. Powerboats had fiberglass damage. According to Daniel, this place had looked like a nuke went off just after the storm.

I decided to anchor instead of picking up a mooring ball. I didn't trust them after what they'd been through. Just beyond the Bridge to Nowhere, there was an anchorage to starboard. I steered us to it. Right in the center of the anchored boats sat *Another Adventure*, Holly's boat. I anchored nearby. I saw Holly on deck, holding up a VHF radio. I switched my radio to channel seventy-two and hailed her.

"We've got to stop meeting like this," I said.

"I thought you were Daniel," she said.

"He's up north," I said. "On the Chesapeake."

"Why didn't he take his boat up there?" she asked.

"No time," I said. "That's what we're doing. Delivering it to him."

"Got time for a visit?"

"Sure, come on over."

She came over and joined us. Brody was okay with it. The two of them had an understanding.

Holly had graciously passed the torch and even encouraged us to love each other. She was a hell of a woman, but she seemed destined to remain single forever.

"I'm sorry about Daniel," she said. "He didn't do a damn thing wrong. He's a great guy."

"What happened?" asked Brody.

"I got so wrapped up in helping out here," she began. "We were raising boats like mad. Everything was so urgent. I kind of got manic about it. In the process I ignored him. I spent all my time with the guys who were helping me."

"Seems like a reasonable enough thing," I said.

"While that was all going down, I decided that he was too young for me," she said. "I've been down that road before. It didn't end well. When he finally brought it up, I told him I didn't have time for some emotional discussion about it. I could see that he was hurt, but he took it like a man."

"That's too bad," said Brody. "But we won't hold it against you. Will we, Breeze?"

"He's a big boy," I said. "Already got him a new girl up north. No big deal."

"When you talk to him," said Holly. "Please tell him I'm sorry."

"You living here now?" I asked.

"Just passing back through on my way to the Bahamas," she said. "Trying to round up crew."

"Stay away from the hippies this time," I said.

"I am a hippie," she said. "We're not all bad."

"Present company exempted," I said. "Good to see you, girl."

"How long are you hanging around?"

I looked at Brody and tried to read her expression. Her face was telling me not to stick around too long. It was as clear as if she'd spoken the words.

"We aren't staying," I said. "We've got a long way to go."

"Have a safe trip," Holly said. "Pass along my best."

"Will do," I said. "Safe travels to you."

She went back to *Another Adventure*, leaving Brody and me alone.

"You read my mind," Brody said.

"As best I could," I said. "What's the deal? You're not jealous, are you?"

"Not at all," she said. "I'm secure in our relationship. I just smelled some upcoming drama. We've had enough of that to last for a while."

"I hear you," I said. "I'm good with moving on right away. We really don't need anything from here."

"You're the captain," she said.

We moved on from Marathon the very next day. There was no urgency to our travel then. We could relax and make day trips from port to port. We stopped at Islamorada and ate dinner at the Lorelei. We anchored in Tarpon Basin behind Key Largo to catch happy hour at Hobo's. We dropped the hook at Key Biscayne just outside No Name Harbor. We'd come full circle since our return from the Bahamas.

My level of paranoia had dropped significantly since we'd left on Daniel's boat. No one could know that it was us aboard. Our phone wouldn't give us away. We only used Brody's tablet on public Wi-Fi. We were ghosts in the vast sea of humanity that was America. I liked it that way.

We worked our way slowly up the east coast, stopping in interesting towns and taking in the sights. We didn't do much sailing during that time. We had to stop for fuel often. Eventually, we made our way to North Myrtle Beach. The boat we were there to see was in Harbourgate Marina in a neighborhood known as Little River. A Holiday Inn Express sat directly across the street. Brody literally begged for us to get a room. She was tired of the cramped quarters of the sailboat. I was too. We booked a suite with a king-sized bed.

We let the broker know we were in town. He advised us that the owner was aboard the boat, and we could walk over and check it out, even though our appointment was for the next day. The owner greeted us with enthusiasm. He was in the market for something bigger. He welcomed us aboard and showed us around. The vessel was an Aquarius aft-cabin motor yacht. The exterior showed well. The interior was plush and luxurious. It had a washer and dryer, large separate shower stalls, and even an electric fireplace. The fridge was full-sized. The air conditioning kept it nice and cool inside. The icemaker on the ample sundeck pumped out ice cubes.

Brody was in love with it. I liked it but remained skeptical. I wasn't sure if I could ever part with *Miss Leap*. Was this boat her replacement? I crawled around in the engine room. I checked bilge compartments. I looked for signs of water intrusion. It appeared to be solid and dry. I went up on the bridge to find thirty-year-old electronics. All of it was beyond outdated. It even still had a Loran. I could do without most of it, but it would require a new GPS or chart plotter.

I stood and gave the boat a chance to speak to me. It didn't talk. I walked around on deck, trying to get a feel for her soul. I sat at the helm to see what it would feel like to pilot her, still waiting for her to communicate to me. I got nothing. I had to admit, it was a nice boat, but something wasn't right. She didn't reach out and grab me. The broker joined us and we chatted for fifteen minutes. Brody was admiring the queen-sized bed in the huge master stateroom.

"I really like this boat," she said.

"Me too," I said. "But I'm not sold yet."

I asked the broker if we could keep the next day's appointment. I needed to think about things, and I may have more questions. He agreed. We shook hands with him and the owner and walked away from it. I took Brody to dinner at a place called Filet's, right on the river.

"What's not to like?" she asked.

"We're going to need a dinghy to get it home," I said.

"We can get a dinghy," she said.

"And a new chart plotter," I said.

"I saw a West Marine just up the road," she said. "Come on, Breeze. It's perfect."

"No boat is perfect," I said. "I need to check out a few things tomorrow."

"You made a promise," she said.

"If the right boat comes along," I said. "I'm just not convinced that this is the right boat."

"Well, I love it."

"Noted."

After dinner, we returned to the hotel room and did something we seldom did. Brody turned on the TV and switched back and forth between news channels. The web of deceit and trickery in Washington had only grown more complicated. Agent Strzok and his mistress discussed an insurance policy against Trump's election. It was something they had cooked up in Andy McCabe's office. The wife of the founder of Fusion GPS had visited the White

House during the time the dossier had first been circulated. Bruce Ohr's wife, who worked for Fusion, had previously worked for the CIA. McCabe was called to testify before Congress behind closed doors. The information that leaked out was damaging to him. There were calls for him to resign. He announced that he would be retiring in a few months, as soon as he was eligible for full retirement benefits. Trump teased on Twitter. "Will he make it that long?"

One of the talking heads read a list of eight people involved in various investigations that had either been fired or reassigned. Chaos reigned at both the FBI and the DOJ. Meanwhile, Mueller still plugged along, endlessly seeking collusion between Trump and the Russians. Trump himself stayed above the fray, seemingly unconcerned. He scored a major victory by getting a tax reform bill through Congress. The Republicans celebrated and then left town for the holidays.

Brody sat there shaking her head. "This should have all come tumbling down already," she said. "Folks should be in jail by now."

"I didn't hear anything about Hillary in all that mess," I said.

"They got an email from McCabe that proves she got special treatment," she said. "It's called an HQ Special."

"Does any of it concern us in any way?" I asked. "If not, I'd just as soon forget all about it."

"I'm long forgotten most likely," she said. "The stuff they're uncovering now is way above my pay grade."

"Turn it off then," I suggested. "We can find better ways to entertain ourselves."

We took advantage of the king-sized bed. Afterwards, we made full use of the big shower stall. The relative luxury of the nice room brought Brody's attention back to buying a nicer boat.

"What else do you need to know about this boat?" she asked.

"I noticed the windlass was designed for rope rode only," I said. "We'll have to replace it. It's going to need an all-chain rode and a bigger anchor."

"Is that something doable?"

"I need to get up under the windlass and see how it's supported," I said.

"What else?"

"Check for soft spots and rotted wood," I said. "A full survey will find that, but if it's soft we won't bother to get a surveyor."

"Why didn't we just stay longer and check it out fully?"

"I didn't want to poke around too hard with the owner watching," I said. "Made me uncomfortable."

"So we go back and dig a little deeper tomorrow," she said. "I hope she checks out."

"We'll see."

We went back the next day and began investigating a little deeper. Unfortunately, the windlass installation was a disaster. It was simply bolted through thin fiberglass with no backing plate or support of any kind. To handle a proper chain windlass, that area would have to be built up and supported with something substantial. I also learned that the bottom hadn't been painted in three years. I had no desire to do the job. It likely had some blisters from staying in the water that long. The bills to make her right were adding up.

I went up on the bridge and took another look at the sad electronics. I could do without radar. *Leap of Faith* didn't have it. I could rip out the old Loran. A new, modern GPS would get us back to the west coast of Florida. I could probably scrounge up a dinghy somewhere, or just buy a cheap one from West Marine. It was a nice enough boat, but I couldn't bring myself to like it.

I gave it one more chance. I put my hands on the wheel and waited for her to speak to me. I tried to feel her spirit.

"Come on, girl," I said. "Tell me you're worthy."

Nothing. I sat in silence for another five minutes. I detected no soul. She didn't have it in her. I couldn't buy that boat. Brody came up and sat beside me.

"I'm giving this thing every chance to feel the love," I said. "But it's not happening."

"She doesn't understand," she offered. "She's been a dock queen all her life. Her owner didn't communicate with her like you do."

"Look, you're asking me to give up a vital piece of my life," I said. "*Miss Leap* is a part of me, and I am part of her. I'm willing to entertain the idea, but not for this boat. It's just not a worthy replacement."

"No boat will ever be worthy," she said. "I see that now."

"We can keep looking," I said. "But I'm done here."

"I'm really not looking forward to the rest of this trip," she said. "That sailboat doesn't suit me at all."

"Especially after a nice hotel room," I said. "You want to jump offshore and make a run for the Chesapeake?"

"Can the boat handle it?"

"It made it to Guatemala and back," I said. "The question is can we take it?"

"How long?"

"Couple of days nonstop," I said. "We're almost to North Carolina now. We can run out Little River and be in the Atlantic in fifteen minutes."

"One more nice night in a big comfy bed," she said.

"I'll check the weather," I said. "We'll slip out of here early in the morning if it looks good."

Fifteen

The little sailboat seemed happy to be in the ocean. She sprang to life when the sails went up. Brody even enjoyed the ride. We had a moderate breeze out of the north, so we sailed northeast for hours. We tacked back towards the coast around noon, making note of the charted shoals to our west. We continued making long tacks, zigging and zagging on an indirect course northward. *Lion's Den* was making seven knots, the same speed that *Leap of Faith* traveled. Brody got the hang of swinging the boom and ducking under it.

As we started our last long tack out to sea and away from the coast before sunset, I took the opportunity to take a nap. All Brody had to do was maintain course for a few hours. I went below and let the sound of the waves lull me to sleep.

Sometime during the evening, those waves changed. The different sounds woke me. I scrambled up on deck to see what was going on. Brody was asleep, hunched over in the cockpit. We'd shifted onto a due west course. The boat was flying towards Bermuda on a beam reach. We were in the Gulf Stream. The waves began to stand up and slam into the hull. I shook Brody awake.

"We've got to reduce sail and head back in," I told her. "We're about to take a beating out here."

"Where are we?"

"In the Stream in a north wind," I said. "It's getting ugly."

She apologized while rubbing her eyes. There wasn't any point in belaboring her mistake. I needed her to snap out of it and help.

"Let's go, Brody," I said. "Reef the main while I bring down the jib."

I slammed my big toe into a stanchion on the way forward. It hurt like hell. I called for Brody to bring us around. As we turned, a wave cleared the bow and swept across the foredeck. I lost my footing and went down. I tasted seawater as I grabbed onto a safety line.

"Hang on, Breeze," shouted Brody.

"Turn us more to the west," I yelled back. "We've got to get out of the Stream."

The jib was still up. We had too much sail flying in those conditions. I crawled forward, leaving a blood trail from my toe. I remembered why I didn't like sailing. I stood long enough to get the sail down, then crawled back to Brody.

"Having fun yet?" I asked.

"I'm so sorry," she said. "I just passed out."

"It will settle down some once we get out of the worst of the current," I told her. "We'll be okay."

I made some adjustments, steering us due west. We weren't headed towards our objective, but we needed to run for calmer waters. The seas gradually subsided to a level we could withstand. I sent Brody below to get some rest. I was disappointed that she'd let me down. She was disappointed that we weren't buying that boat. We were both going to have to get over our disappointment. Shit would work out.

On the night watch all alone, I recounted the events of the past few months. Hurricane Irma had turned our lives upside down, but we'd recovered. The FBI interfered in our lives in a big way, but we'd resolved the matter. It wasn't the first time that outside events had made my decisions for me, but I didn't like it. It was time to put that all behind us and start living the life that we chose for ourselves. It was not a good time to consider parting with *Miss Leap*. It would be a step too far. Maybe someday, the right boat would present itself, but I needed her stability in my life just then. She was my rock, my constant loyal companion. Brody would have to understand.

Eventually, we made it to the Chesapeake. After a brief encounter with a submarine at the Bay Bridge Tunnel, we entered the relative calm of the bay. Fishing boats dotted the rock piles and pilings all along the structure. The fishermen were all bundled up against the cold. Brody and I were freezing. We'd brought what little warm clothing we had, but it wasn't enough. An arctic front had dropped down from Canada and sent the temperatures plummeting. I aimed for Kiptopeke. We anchored just outside the concrete ships and tried to get warm. I fired up the propane stove while Brody closed up anything that might let the heat escape. We pulled the blanket off the bunk and huddled under it.

"I've had enough of this shit," said Brody. "First this uncomfortable little boat and now the cold. Why are we doing this again?"

"To help Daniel," I reminded her. "Our friend."

"He can have this damn boat," she said. "I'm really starting to hate it."

"A few more days and we'll give it back to him," I said. "We can make it a few more days."

"Get me back to Florida," she said. "My blood has gotten too thin for this weather."

"I'm not liking it too much either," I said. "But it's what we have to endure to complete our mission."

"Endeavor to persevere," she said. "I'd rather be lying by the pool."

"Or on a beach," I said. "We'll be back soon enough. We'll appreciate it that much more."

The little stove was doing its job. Our body heat combined under the blanket to ward off the shivers. We fell asleep in each other's arms, dreaming of warmer places. It was rather pleasant, considering the circumstances. Our sleep was interrupted in the morning by the sound of outboard motors. The fishermen were coming out of the nearby boat ramp and running full tilt towards the bridge. The bite must have really been hot. Otherwise, it was too damn cold to go fishing.

I turned off the stove and stuck my head outside. The fishermen probably thought it was too damn cold to spend the night on a sailboat. The day was bright but the winds were light. We'd have to motor north. I knew Brody wanted to get this over with, so I cranked up the diesel. She came out wrapped in the blanket and handed me a cup of coffee.

"I won't raise the sails unless we get some wind," I told her. "You can stay below and keep warm if you like."

"I think I will," she said. "At least until the sun gets up higher."

"You go ahead," I said. "I've got this."

We cruised north along the eastern shore of Virginia past Cape Charles. I steered us past the mouth of Nassawadox Creek, then swung away from shore to avoid shallow water. It took most of the day to make it to Occohannock Creek. I could have continued, but I was so cold I decided to quit and seek warmth. Brody had the stove going again. She was under the blanket and not looking pleased.

"We didn't make it very far did we?" she asked. "It's going to take more than two days."

"Unless you want to run through the night," I said.

"Not a chance," she replied. "But I'm doing this under protest. We're going to freeze to death up here."

"We're probably not going to die," I said.

"Probably?" she asked. "Jesus, Breeze. I'd rather be fending off pirates in the Caribbean than freezing my ass off."

"I can arrange that if you like," I said.

"No thanks," she said. "Just get me back to Florida."

I checked out our propane supply before going to sleep. It wouldn't last much longer at the rate we were burning it. I got the interior warmed up and shut it down for the evening. Within two hours it was too cold inside to survive. The outside temperature must have been near zero. I shook the propane tank again. I guessed we had enough to make it through the night, and part of the next night. I turned the stove back on.

The next day was no warmer. A good breeze lowered the wind chill even more but allowed us to put up the sails. With the motor running and the sails up, we made eight knots. After a long day, we approached the mouth of the Choptank River. I thought maybe we should just keep on going.

"What do you want to do?" I asked Brody.

"Turn on the heat," she said. "As soon as the sun goes down we're in trouble."

"We can make it by morning," I said.

"You can't sit out here all night," she said. "Seriously."

"I don't think our gas is going to last the night," I said. "We'll freeze anyway."

"I'm calling you bad names in my head right now," she said. "Shit, Breeze. What were you thinking?"

"I certainly wasn't thinking that it would be zero degrees," I said.

"Let's drop anchor and get warm," she said. "We'll keep it on low. Maybe it will last."

I found a spot just inside the river at Black Walnut Point. Brody had the stove going before I got the anchor set. On the low setting, it barely made a dent in the cold. The condensation that formed on the windows started to freeze. We could see our breath. I'd been through hard times. I'd been beaten. I'd been hungry. I'd been mosquito bitten to the point of insanity. None of that compared to the bone-crushing cold we felt that night. It was bad enough for me, but I'd brought Brody into it as well. Her navigational error out in the Atlantic was a minor nuisance compared to the cold we experienced.

Before daylight, the propane ran out. What little warmth the stove had provided dissipated rapidly. Brody began to cry. Her eyes begged for mercy. I tried to recall what little I knew of the area. I remembered a marina of sorts a little further inside the river. I checked the charts and learned that we drew too much water to make it. We could lower the dinghy but I wasn't sure we'd survive the trip. We'd get wet on the way in. I checked the charts further north. There was shelter at Kent Narrows, but that was so close to Rock Hall there was no point in stopping.

I fired up the engine and let it idle for a few minutes. I could feel some heat working its way up through the floorboards.

"Stay under the blanket," I told Brody. "I'll pull the anchor."

"It's not light yet," she said.

"There's no crab pots this time of year," I said. "The engine will give us some heat. We'll be there before the marina closes."

I thought my fingers would fall off as I pulled up the anchor chain. I put my hands in my pockets and steered with my elbows until we got back out in the bay. Ice formed on my mustache and eyelids. After an hour I couldn't take it anymore. I lashed the wheel in place and went below. The engine warmed our hot water tank while underway. I ran my hands under hot water, feeling them tingle. I splashed hot water on my face. Brody stayed under the blanket.

"You're one crazy son of a bitch," she said. "I can't believe we're doing this."

"It will all be over soon," I said.

I dried off and fashioned some makeshift mittens out of hand towels. I wrapped a bath towel around my face and went back outside. The sun came up and raised the temperature out of the single digits. We motored north. The route 50 bridge was a welcome sight. There were no fishermen out that day. I didn't see a single boat on the bay. I was the only crazy one out there.

I had Brody call Daniel to let him know we'd be arriving soon. I hailed the marina on the radio. It took three tries before someone answered. I took it they weren't used to having traffic on cold winter days. The dock master informed me of a thin sheet of ice inside the harbor. He said I shouldn't have any trouble breaking through it. He'd be there to grab lines when we came in. Daniel said he was leaving for Rock Hall immediately.

We were one mile out when the engine quit.

I cranked it over but it wouldn't restart. I could clearly see the entrance to Rock Hall Harbor. The marina was just inside the jetty to the left. There was ice on the rip rap that formed the sea wall. I went forward to find the roller furling covered in ice. I couldn't budge it to raise the jib. I tried the main. Everything was frozen solid from the sea spray. We drifted, helpless. I called the dock master again. There was no vessel immediately available to come to our aid. He could call a tow boat for us, but they'd be coming from home and might be a while. He suggested I drop the anchor and wait.

I was in no mood to sit for a few hours waiting for help. I was bone-cold and frustrated beyond the breaking point. I knew that Brody would be in full mutiny soon. I had to do something. I went below and filled our biggest cooking pot with hot water. I dumped it on the frozen furling. Most of the ice melted away but it still wouldn't move. I repeated the process until it broke free. I raised half the jib and we started to move. I continued to work it back and forth to prevent it from refreezing. I called the marina again.

"I'm coming in under a small sail," I said. "I'll need hands to stop us."

"You're out of your mind, sailor," he said. "I hope you've got good insurance."

There was no insurance. There was only my limited sailing ability. I'd never attempted such a maneuver. I wasn't even sure how I was going to do it. I just knew that we were heading in.

"What's going on?" Asked Brody.

"You want to drop the sail or steer?" I asked her.

"We're sailing into the slip?" she asked. "You are nuts."

"We can do this," I said. "But I need your help."

"I'll steer," she said. "Tell me what to do."

219

"Once inside the jetty," I began. "Take a nice easy turn to the left. Try to keep your momentum. When I spot the slip, I'll point it out. Wait until the last second and turn hard left. I'll drop the sail. That should slow us down."

"How do we stop?" she asked.

It was a damn good question. I hoped that we'd have help on the dock, but I couldn't count on it. How were we going to stop? I tied one line to a bow cleat. I tied a line to the starboard stern and the port stern.

"As we enter the slip I'll drop the sail and run back here with you," I said. "We each try to lasso a piling as we go by. We'll only get one shot at it, but maybe one of us will score."

"Good grief," she said. "Yippee ki-yay."

"Just put a big loop in the end and toss it over the piling," I said.

We ignored the cold after that. The game was on. There was a decent chance that we'd smash into the dock, or worse, another boat. I held out for the chance that one of us would rope a piling and save the day. If we weren't going too fast, it wouldn't be impossible.

We crawled into the harbor entrance at three knots. Brody turned us to port in a slow arc.

We slowed to two knots. We crept along until I saw the dock master waving to us. I pointed him out to Brody.

"I see it," she said. "Say when."

We inched closer. We got even with the first piling when I yelled to Brody.

"Turn it over hard now," I said.

She spun the wheel hard to port. I dropped the sail to the foredeck. Our bow was aiming directly into the slip, but we lost all forward motion. I had a thirty-foot line on the bow. The dock master stood forty feet in front of me. He was too far to throw a line to. We were dead in the water.

I spied those pilings that I'd told Brody to lasso. They were in front of us, but close. I grabbed a line from the stern and brought it forward. Brody saw what I was doing and followed my lead. We both went forward and tried to toss our rope on a piling. We both missed on the first attempt. We tried again and failed. On the third try, I managed to get most of a loop on the starboard side piling. I flicked and wiggled the line until it fell over the top of the post. I had it. I pulled us forward and gave us enough forward motion to make it the rest of the way. I ran back with my line and stopped us with a stern cleat. The guy on the dock fended off our bow. Brody secured the port side.

"We did it," she said.

"I'll be a son of a bitch," the dock master said.

"Is it warm in your office?" I asked. "We're dying out here."

"Come on inside," he said. "I'll get some coffee going. Never seen nothing like it."

We quickly finished securing the boat and scurried up the dock to his office. Warm forced air was coming out of the vents. A small open flame propane heater glowed on the wall. Brody stood in front of it with her hands inches from the flame.

"Don't give me that shit works out pep talk," she said. "This shit did not work out."

"We're here, aren't we?" I said. "Safe and sound, if not a little frozen."

"I don't think I'll ever thaw out," she said. "And I sure as hell don't want to try any more stunts like that."

"You did great," I said. "You're a natural."

"No I'm not," she said. "We were lucky as hell. Never is too soon to put me on another sailboat, or to freeze my ass off."

"I can't blame you," I said. "As soon as Daniel gets here we'll make arrangements to get home."

"You owe me another hotel room," she said. "With a hot tub."

"Deal."

The warmth of the marina office cured some of our ills. Our body temperatures returned to normal. The hot coffee cleared our minds. Our distaste for the situation we found ourselves in remained. We had survived, but we were still twelve hundred miles from the Florida sun. Brody was disgusted with me. The dock master kept looking at his watch.

Daniel finally arrived late in the afternoon.

"Holy shit, you two," he said. "It's cold as balls out."

"The engine isn't running, but we got her here," I told him.

"What's wrong with it?" he asked.

"I wouldn't be surprised if the fuel started to gel from the cold," I said. "Wait until it warms up. If it starts and runs, put some additive in the fuel tank."

"She's not used to this weather," he said.

"Neither are we," said Brody. "You're welcome."

"Thanks a ton," he said. "But you guys volunteered if you remember."

"Breeze volunteered," she said, giving me the evil eye.

"Where are you staying?" I asked Daniel.

"Ocean City," he said. "Long ride."

"Why did you choose Rock Hall?" I asked.

"Sailing is better over here," he said. "I plan to spend weekends on the boat. It will be a nice getaway."

"In the summertime," said Brody. "Do you mind getting us to a hotel tonight?"

"We can stop in Dover," he said. "It's about an hour away. How are you getting back to Florida?"

"Fly, I guess," I said. "Kent Narrows would be closer to the airport in Baltimore. You can take Route 50 back down to Ocean City."

"That'll work," he said. "You ready to roll?"

"More than ready," said Brody.

We drove to the Hilton Garden Inn in Grasonville. Directly beside it was the Jetty Dock Bar, where I'd married my wife, Laura. The place was deserted due to the cold. Not much tourism goes on there during the winter. It did bring back memories though. Brody's foul mood didn't help matters. I was deep in the doghouse.

We both took long, hot showers. Brody made arrangements to get us to the airport the next day. We ate a nice meal at the Fisherman's Inn. I picked up a six-pack and a pint of rum, which we shared. The booze cut the tension between us.

"I still can't believe we put that boat in the slip without an engine," she said. "What made you think we could manage that?"

"I think we'd all be surprised at what we could do if we just tried," I said. "We don't try it because there's no need to. We take for granted that everything is always going to be as it should be. That's clearly not the case. I guess I'm more accustomed to making do with what I've got than most people."

"You're quick to improvise," she said. "I'll give you that much."

"Put that on my tombstone," I said. "Here lies Breeze. He was quick to improvise."

"You know what I mean," she said. "When presented with a problem, you figure it out. You always seem to overcome."

"What else is there to do?"

"It was just different in the real world," she said. "All sorts of problems go unsolved every day."

"Maybe that's why it sucks so much," I said. "Just leave me alone in my little knothole. I'll find simple solutions to my simple problems."

"Yet you're far from a simple man," she said. "So much potential. You could have been anything."

"Maybe once," I said. "But that world beat me down. All the unnecessary complications that we've imposed upon society, all the constant chaos, rules and regulations...I had to break away from it or lose my sanity."

"Which is the sanest thing I've ever heard a man say," she said. "I'm understanding you more and more. I can see how you got here. Most people will never muster the guts to take the leap."

"If everyone was doing it, I'd have to find another way," I said.

"That's not going to happen," she said. "You're safe. Folks are too conditioned to know better."

"Yet here you are," I said. "Against every rational argument. You're here with me."

"It's you and me, Breeze," she said. "And *Miss Leap.*"

Daniel stayed at the hotel that night too. We all met for the free continental breakfast in the morning.

"If you guys ever need anything," he said. "Anything at all, I can be down there in twenty-four hours."

"Just take care of that boat," I said. "We went through a lot getting her up here."

"And that girlfriend of yours," said Brody. "What's her name again?"

"Dalyn," he said. "And she's almost as pretty as you Brody."

"You're sweet," she said. "And full of shit, but I appreciate the compliment."

"When you can get the time off, bring her down for a visit," I said.

"I'll do that," he said. "Thanks for everything, Breeze. Yet again."

"Don't sweat it, kid," I said. "Just make us proud."

"I will," he said. "I won't let you down."

We parted ways with our young friend. Our ride to the airport arrived right on time. We were dropped off at BWI. We had no reservation. Brody went to three different counters before finding someone who would accept cash for our tickets. A few hours later, we boarded a Spirit Airlines flight to Fort Myers. We touched down late in the afternoon and found a shuttle service to take us to the marina. Just like that, we were back onboard *Leap of Faith*. We went straight to our bunk, made love, and slept the sleep of the saved and thankful.

Sixteen

Our tribulations were behind us. All we had to endure was the heat of the Florida sun, a few tourists that invaded our peaceful pool, and the white-haired snowbirds that invaded the grocery stores and restaurants. Whenever we had our fill of people, we'd anchor out in Pelican Bay and enjoy the solitude for a few days or weeks. The dolphins still came to visit. The manatees still popped their noses above the surface to breathe. White pelicans by the scores chased fish around the bay.

Brody paid less attention to what was going on in Washington. The previous months faded from our memory. I was forgiven for our arctic excursion to the Chesapeake. There was no more talk of buying a new boat. We collected sand dollars by the dozens. We waded hand in hand in the clear Gulf waters. My blood pressure reacted favorably. We ate well, slept well, and had good sex.

For the first time in years, I didn't itch for adventure. I felt that Brody's love and companionship were curing my wanderlust. My dream had been fulfilled. There was no longer a desperate need to search for happiness in some exotic port. I had found it right there in Pelican Bay with Brody. I couldn't thank her enough.

I felt rested and healthy so I decided to work on my fitness. There's only so much lying on a beach that a man can handle. I started with long brisk walks before graduating to jogging in the sand. I swam in the Gulf for increasing distances. I found a sea grape tree with a branch that was perfect for pull-ups. We ate more fish and fruit. Since my hypertension diagnosis, I'd developed all sorts of doubts about my abilities. I feared getting old. I worried about every small ache and pain. After two months of paying more attention to my physical readiness, the haze lifted. I was sharper in body and mind. I enjoyed the sights, sounds, and tastes more.

I still drank my beer and the occasional nip of rum. Brody and I would sit and watch the sunset with our drink of choice. The days slipped by quickly. We were happy. *Miss Leap* was happy too until we got a call from Captain Fred.

"I've got a favor to ask, Breeze," he said. "I don't reckon you'll want to say no to me."

"Wouldn't dream of it," I said. "What do you need?"

"I want to get *Incognito* back down to the Exumas," he said. "I might have to fly in and out during the trip. I need a competent captain to keep her moving when I'm gone."

That actually sounded like fun, except that we'd have to leave *Leap of Faith* behind. It took her a month to get over her snit the last time we'd abandoned her.

"Brody and I can help," I said. "When are you thinking?"

"As soon as you can get your salty ass down here," he said. "I'm at the Pink Shell."

"We can be there tomorrow," I said. "Anything you need."

"Good boy," he said. "See you then."

I had no choice in the matter. I owed him big time. I'd promised that I'd help him whenever he needed with whatever he needed. He was calling in the favor. I had to respond. That's just the way it is. I could think of worse ways to repay him. Taking his big yacht down through the Bahamas was easy duty. Brody could enjoy the luxuries that came with it on the way. She'd been listening to my side of the conversation. I filled her in on the rest.

"We're taking Captain Fred's boat down through the Bahamas to George Town," I told her.

"Sweet," she said. "How'd you arrange that?"

"I'm helping him out," I said. "Small price to pay."

"I'll say," she said. "It will be fun."

We left for Fort Myers Beach early the next day. The water was still pretty, but we started seeing dead fish below the Captiva Pass. Red tide had arrived off the coast of Sanibel and Captiva. If it worked its way north, it was a good time to vacate the area. Nothing like the smell of rotting fish to disturb the evening sunset.

We waved to Fred as we passed his boat, before picking up a mooring ball. We paid for a month, asked Diver Dan to keep an eye on our boat, and took the dinghy to the Pink Shell.

Captain Fred had something yummy smelling on the grill. He handed us each a beer.

"I appreciate this," he said. "I certainly appreciate your lady friend. It will be nice to have her aboard."

"We appreciate your hospitality," I said. "Just keep your hands to yourself, old man."

"Look but don't touch," he says. Some gratitude."

"I've grown more than partial to her," I said. "Just so you know."

"I expected as much," he said. "It's about time."

We ate a fine meal as Captain Fred explained his itinerary. His wife would be flying to George Town at a later date. He had multiple business transactions in the fire and may have to fly out at any time. We'd stay close to islands with airports as we worked our way south. Brody and I would continue to travel in his absence, picking him up elsewhere, or meeting him in George Town, if necessary. He'd fly us back when we were ready to leave. We'd be welcome to stay as long as we liked. It was a dream trip. It certainly wasn't work. I couldn't think of an easier way to repay a favor.

Before our departure, Captain Fred walked me through the engine room. It was completely lined with diamond plate. Each tool in the stainless cabinet was numbered. Hatteras sent a man from the Carolinas to service the engines and everything he needed was in that tool cabinet. The engines were 870 horsepower Detroits for a total of 1740 horses. Fifty gallons of oil was constantly circulated, heated and polished twenty-four hours per day. The vessel held fifteen hundred gallons of diesel fuel and three-hundred, forty-five gallons of water. The holding tanks totaled over one-hundred gallons.

"She'll push thirty knots in a pinch," said Fred. "But then she sucks fuel like it's going through a fire hose."

"It's not like you don't have the money," I said.

"I don't want to run out before we get where we're going," he explained. "We won't be passing too many fuel docks. Keep her around twelve knots unless we get pushed for time."

We went to the upper helm to go over the controls.

"All these gauges have a corresponding alarm," he said. "It's idiot proof, but close quarters maneuvering takes some getting used to."

He bumped the bow thruster right and left to show me how it worked.

"Lots of torque," he said. "Go to neutral for slow. Even idle speed is too fast inside marinas. Bump her in and out of gear to maintain control."

"Gotcha," I said. "I don't have that issue on my boat."

"We'll be running twice as fast as you're used to," he said. "And that's leaving plenty in reserve."

"I can handle boats," I said. "I love boats."

"He talks to them," Brody chimed in. "He's the boat whisperer."

I'd been aboard *Incognito* several times. I knew a bit about her. She'd spent several years in the Bahamas previously. Back in the states, Captain Fred liked to move around from marina to marina. It got used. It got driven from time to time. Fred handled her well and expected me to do the same. I was confident that I could live up to his expectations.

"May I?" I asked, holding my finger over one of the start buttons.

"Be my guest," said Fred.

The port engine fired to life with a deep rumble. The starboard engine did the same. I listened to their sounds. I felt their vibrations. I patted the dashboard.

"We're going to get along just fine," I told her.

I sensed her approval. She was telling me that she was ready for an adventure.

"Test spin?" I asked.

"You better let me back her away from the dock," he said. "Then you can take over."

"I've got to learn sooner or later," I said, trying not to sound offended.

"If you feel comfortable," he said. "Me and Brody will toss the lines."

I'll admit I was slightly anxious. There was a strong cross-current running past the docks. It was a strange boat to me. I didn't know how it would respond. I didn't let that stop me. I eased both shifters in reverse and we eased out of the slip. When the current pushed us, I adjusted. I managed not to bang the pilings on the way out. We turned on a pivot once clear. I throttled up in forward and eased us towards the pass. I held her below six knots until we left the no-wake zone, then ran her up to twelve. I took us out into the Gulf for a few miles before turning around.

"You want me to dock her?" asked Fred.

"Let me try," I said. "Feel free to advise me."

I slowed to less than a crawl well before the slip. The current would carry us so I started my turn early. I nudged each shifter in and out of gear, aligning the bow with the right-side piling. As I bumped into forward, the current helped to center us. We came to a stop, lines were thrown, and I shut her down. It was like I was intimate with the boat and the way it handled, smooth as silk.

"Good job, captain," said Brody.

"Good job, mate," I said.

"Good job, *Incognito*," we both said.

"Looks like I made a good choice," said Captain Fred. "But there's another reason I've got you aboard."

"What's that?" I asked.

"Let's go down to the salon," He said. "I've got some things to tell you."

The three of us reconvened below, safe from surveillance inside Fred's protective bubble.

"Why do I have a bad feeling about this?" I asked.

"I'll get straight to the point," he said. "I received a tip from within the FBI."

"Concerning Brody?" I asked. "I thought that was all behind us now."

"As did I," he said. "But apparently someone has gone rogue."

"Gone rogue how?" Brody asked.

"Someone ordered a hit on you," he said. "The contractor is outside of the FBI."

"This has got to be some kind of sick joke," she said. "Please tell me this isn't real."

"Director Wray claims no knowledge," he said. "Apparently he just found out about it. He assured me that the gunman has no access to the tools available to the Bureau. He's a freelancer. Someone unnamed within the FBI took it upon themselves to hire him."

"Shit, Fred," I said. "Why didn't you tell us on the phone? We would have been a bit more alert."

"I'm not sure we can continue to trust that avenue of communication," he said. "You've had it for too long. I knew you'd come running. I've got you over a barrel. You owe me."

"So I'm not really doing you a favor," I said. "You're saving my ass yet again."

"And Brody's," he said. "But there are other considerations that may require your services."

"There's more?" I asked. "I was thinking this would be a nice little vacation for us."

"Listen, you're safe aboard this vessel while I'm aboard," he said. "No one would tolerate having me as a witness. It would be a death sentence."

"Why not kill you too?" I asked. "Collateral damage."

"No offense," he said. "But hired assassins won't take a job to whack someone of my stature. They'd never get work again. You, on the other hand, are a nobody. They could take you out, Brody too, without anyone ever knowing. No loose ends."

"My anonymity makes me an inviting target," I said.

"Brody is the target," he said. "But we can assume you're on the work order as well."

"Why can't Wray recall this guy?" I asked.

"He's underground," he answered. "And Wray didn't hire him."

"So there's a hired gun out there somewhere," I said. "Just waiting for a chance to put a few bullets in our heads?"

"That seems to be the case," he said. "Sorry to be the bearer of bad news."

"Worst news ever," said Brody. "Will this ever end?"

"Not unless the assassin gives up, or is eliminated," said Fred. "For now, we're putting some distance between him and you. Stay aboard as long as you like."

"What about our boat?" I asked.

"I know you don't want to hear this," he began. "But it would be best to leave it behind. Give it away, whatever. It is the most important identifier. It will be the death of you, son."

"That's not going to happen," I told him.

"If you wish, we'll find you a new vessel in the Bahamas," he said. "Something more suitable for the lady. Something more luxurious."

"No, no and no," I said. "Brody and I will just go back to our boat right now. Take our chances."

"Breeze?" said Brody.

"You don't want to do that," said Fred. "I'm calling in all the favors I've ever done for you. You don't want to say no."

"But I'm not helping you," I said. "In fact, we'll be a hindrance."

"Those other considerations I mentioned," he said. "You'll be earning your keep."

"I forgot about that," I said. "What exactly are those other considerations?"

He walked around the salon, checking switches and lights. He opened a hidden cabinet to reveal a collection of sophisticated looking computers and electronics.

"Corporate espionage," he said. "Back in the old days, that meant spies. Planted hires to your company that stole proprietary information. Your competitors needed to know what you were up to or how you planned to accomplish your goals. These days that's all the purview of hackers. Anything having to do with my business interests goes through this impenetrable system. I use normal devices for personal matters, just to give them something to read or listen to."

"What's that got to do with us?" I asked.

"They've not been successful in their attempts to penetrate my system," he said. "The only way for them to get what's on these hard drives is to steal them. They'd have to physically remove these machines from my boat."

"That's not likely to happen," I said.

"Not in the marina," he said. "Not when I'm aboard. But we're taking a trip, and I expect I won't be aboard for parts of it. That's when they'd make their move."

"Are you just being super cautious, or do you have reason to believe that an attempt is being planned?"

"Rumors here, whispers there," he said. "I can't discount any of it."

"You'd be better off hiring professionals," I said.

"And have one of them be the guy who's going to steal my shit?" he said. "I trust you, Breeze. You handled this boat like you've driven it a hundred times. I've known you to be a tough operator. You're resourceful. Brody was FBI. You're the team I've chosen."

I got up and paced around. I looked at Brody. She shrugged. I was not going to totally abandon *Miss Leap*, but I had to help Captain Fred. I'd figure out how to rescue my boat later.

"Weapons?" I asked.

"I showed you the port-side tool cabinet," he said. "The starboard side is the gun locker."

"What's all this worth?" I asked. "Just out of curiosity."

"Billions," he said. "It's as valuable as Bitcoin."

"What the hell is Bitcoin?" I asked.

"Your innocence is charming sometimes," said Brody. "Other times I wish you knew more about what was going on in the world."

"Digital currency," said Fred. "Not controlled by any government or bank."

"What happens when all the computers crash?" I asked. "I wouldn't trust that for a second."

"Immaterial," he said. "It's not what I'm working on."

"How long do your assets need protection?" I asked. "We can't stay aboard forever."

"By the time we reach George Town, or very soon after, this deal should take place," he said. "There will be no point in stealing my equipment after that. Everything will be made public. My anticipated flights will be to dot the i's and cross the t's. It's nearly over."

"Meanwhile, your floating fortress of information and secure communications will be cruising the calm blue waters of the Bahamas, away from prying eyes and petty thieves."

"There will be critical moments," he said. "We'll need to fuel up in Nassau. I'll probably top off again at Staniel Cay. That's when we'll be vulnerable."

"Where will you stay once we reach George Town?" I asked.

"Redshanks," he said. "It's very private as you know."

"No internet back there," I said. "Cell phones barely work."

"I've got my own secure satellite connections," he said. "This ain't no Mickey Mouse operation."

"Brody?" I said. "What do you think?"

She got up and walked over to me. She stuck one finger in my chest.

"You wouldn't part with *Leap of Faith* in order to buy me a nicer boat," she said. "Now you're leaving her behind to help your friend Fred."

"Your friend too," I said. "Remember what he's done for you. Besides, I won't abandon *Leap*. We'll come back for her after this is over."

"Where a fucking hitman will be waiting for us," she said, stabbing me with that finger.

"We dodged him by going to the Chesapeake," I said. "Now we'll be dodging him by going to the Bahamas."

"But our boat is just sitting there for anyone to see," she said. "He could move onto it for all we know. Maybe he'll be cooking bacon and eggs when we show up."

"Diver Dan wouldn't let that happen," I said. "We've got eyes on the boat."

"Listen to me, Breeze," she said. "There's a goddamn assassin looking for us. Shouldn't that be our first priority? Instead, you want to take a luxury cruise. Just blow it off. Wing it. I can't handle things that way."

"I'm open to other suggestions," I said.

It was her turn to pace the floor. She went back and forth a few times before stopping. She chewed a fingernail and tapped another finger to her temple. She resumed pacing. Finally, she stopped and threw her hands in the air.

"I don't know what to do," she said. "Short of forgetting all of this, changing our names and moving to Podunk, Idaho."

"That doesn't sound very appealing," I said.

"Neither does being dead."

I pulled her to me and held her.

"It will be okay," I said. "I'll figure something out."

"It's life or death this time, Breeze," she said. "Put that brain of yours to work."

Seventeen

It was hard not to envision some shadowy figure emerging from some dark place and popping a couple rounds into us with a silenced weapon. Captain Fred felt certain that a hired killer wouldn't make a move on his boat. I felt safer running away, even though people at the FBI knew of our association with Fred. Several times in my life, running had been the best solution. We'd have to come back eventually, but for the time being, I sensed no immediate threat.

I was behind the wheel for most of the trip. Captain Fred worked his phones and sent his emails. Brody toured the boat at least a dozen times. I asked her what she was up to.

"Familiarizing myself with our turf," she said. "Identifying defensive positions. Figuring out lines of fire."

"What's our weapons stash look like?" I asked.

"Ample assortment," she said. "We need to distribute what we have to convenient places. If we're attacked they won't do us any good locked up below. We need to be able to return fire from up here, from the back deck, and from the bow if necessary. We'll need reserve pieces down below, in case we're forced to fall back and take cover."

"See how much ammo we have," I said. "Make sure everything is in firing condition."

"On it," she said.

I really wasn't expecting the type of trouble Brody was preparing for, but it gave her something to do. She was much better with weapons than I was. She was trained in tactics. I tended to fly by the seat of my pants, which sometimes drove her crazy. Might as well put her skills to good use. I concentrated on running the boat, which basically ran itself. The chart plotter was tied into the autopilot. All I had to do was enter our course and keep watch. The machinery did the rest. Still, I continued to watch gauges and maintain a feel for how things were running. It was a fine vessel. It probably cost more than all the money I'd ever had in my life. It was a privilege to operate.

I took back manual control of navigation when we approached Miami. The combination of heavy recreational and commercial traffic made it a busy place. Cruise ships and freighters jockeyed for space. Harbor control tried to maintain some semblance of order. Fred guided me into a fuel dock specializing in larger yachts. His seventy-footer was among the smaller vessels in attendance. He didn't ask to take over the helm. He let me approach the dock, standing by if I needed assistance. I didn't.

We took on fuel and topped off the water tanks. Brody stood guard. Her personal weapon rode in a holster on her hip. Fred wanted to get a marina slip for the night. Brody and I disagreed. We'd feel safer at anchor. I took the boat back south to Key Biscayne, and we dropped the hook just outside No Name Harbor for the night. By the time I got the anchor set, Fred had the grill fired up.

We ate a gourmet meal accompanied by an expensive wine. Brody seemed to appreciate the wine. I couldn't tell the difference between that and Boone's Farm, but it was nice to be catered to by someone as rich and powerful as Captain Fred. Brody and I thanked him several times, even going as far as suggesting that hamburgers or hot dogs would be good enough for us.

"Nonsense," he said. "You can eat that crap when I'm not here, but we'll have nothing but the best when I'm aboard."

I went over various weather reports that night. The forecasted wind and waves would be no problem for *Incognito*. Fred warned me about the lack of maneuvering room at Bimini, where he planned to check in. I asked him about fuel burn and calculated that we'd have no problem bypassing Bimini and heading straight to Chub Cay. It was a short hop to Nassau from there. He agreed. We retired to our staterooms for the night.

Brody and I shared a king-sized bed covered in zillion-count sheets and a silky down comforter.

"Is it okay for us to get the sheets dirty?" I asked. "If you know what I mean."

"There's a laundry room on board," she said. "What the hell?"

We proceeded to dirty the sheets.

Crossing the Gulf Stream was a snap in Fred's boat. It only took us four hours to clear Gun

Cay. We crossed the Bahama Banks to Chub in no time at all. The marina there was accustomed to larger vessels. The fuel dock was easily accessible. We ate a dinner of cracked conch in the Chub Cay Club. Waitstaff and dockhands fell all over themselves to be helpful and pleasant. It was a treatment that I was not used to. Fred tipped them all generously.

In preparation for our arrival in Nassau, Brody had drawn up a diagram of the boat. She marked where each weapon was stored, and how much ammo was with it. All weapons were fully loaded and operational. The three of us did a walk-through, verifying our arsenal at each location. Fred was a Marine. Brody was FBI. I was clearly the least capable member of the crew when it came to shooting, but I had some experience handling firearms. I'd used a shotgun to good effect on several occasions. That's what I chose to keep on the bridge.

The threat still didn't seem real to me. I just couldn't imagine some shifty characters attacking us or trying to sneak aboard. It all seemed absurd. Fred had a security system, including cameras and alarms. We were prepared to physically confront up to a half-dozen invaders. The enemy better bring ten men or more, or be awfully tricky. Still, I took Brody's instructions seriously. If bullets started flying, I'd do my part.

I'd accepted the role of full-time captain. Fred mostly stayed below, working his corporate magic. We pulled out of Chub mid-morning en route to Nassau. The trip took a mere three hours.

"Nassau Harbor Control, Nassau Harbor Control," I called on the radio. "This is the motor vessel *Incognito* requesting permission to transit the harbor."

"*Incognito*, this is harbor control," came the reply. "What is your destination?"

"Atlantis Marina, in Paradise Lake," I answered.

"Very good, captain," he said. "May I have your documentation numbers please?"

"U.S. 1232081," I said.

"How many passengers on board?"

"Three, counting myself."

"Permission granted," he said. "Enjoy your visit."

I piloted around a cruise ship leaving the harbor and aimed for Potters Cay. There I swung to port, went under a tall bridge and entered Paradise Lake where the marina sat in its northwest corner. I carefully steered us in, hailing the marina as we went. I got our slip assignment and saw several dockhands scramble down the dock to catch our lines. The place was filled with mega-yachts, some of which put our vessel to shame. It must have been quite expensive, but it was Fred's money so what did I care? It was directly adjacent to Atlantis Casino, where Fred wanted to do some gambling. Brody and I would stay behind to guard the boat. I had no interest in gambling anyway. Games of chance were not my forte. If the contest involved reason and logic, a contestant stood a chance to win. Games requiring only luck were all set up to vastly favor the house. Sure, some lucky sucker won big occasionally, but overall the casino always came out on top.

There was no wind or current inside the marina. Docking was relatively simple. The crew on the dock did a good job securing us. A tall man in a sport coat greeted us when the dockhands were finished. I didn't like the looks of him. Two more men in the same coat stood behind him. I was immediately suspicious.

"Permission to come aboard, captain," the man asked.

"Not granted," I said.

We hadn't yet lowered a gangplank or ladder to the dock.

"Just a friendly visit from Customs and Immigration," he said. "We'll be happy to expedite your paperwork and get you on your way."

I was familiar with Bahamian Customs. They never sent three men. They also didn't magically appear at dockside just as you arrived. They couldn't station men at every marina in the Bahamas just to wait for the next boat to arrive.

"What's going on?" asked Brody.

"I figure the harbormaster tipped them off," I said. "Alert Fred."

I had seriously doubted we'd encounter whoever might want to steal Fred's computer equipment. I'd been wrong. I stalled to give Brody time.

"I'm going to need to see some ID," I said.

The two men in the back looked at each other nervously. I thought I caught a glimpse of a holster on one of them. The head man walked to the stern of the boat. His henchmen followed. It was their intention to board us via the swim platform. It was a really bad idea.

Brody and Captain Fred met them with weapons drawn. I walked to the rear of the bridge and pointed my shotgun down at them. They were looking down the barrel of three weapons. They hadn't even drawn theirs yet.

"I suggest you abandon whatever ideas you had about boarding our vessel," I said. "You wouldn't want a bunch of holes in that nice jacket would you?"

"You seem to have the upper hand," he said. "We will leave quietly."

"Smart move," I said. "I've got a good look at all three of you. I'll be calling the police in a few minutes to give them your descriptions. Leaving the island might be a good idea."

"No need to involve the police," he said. "We just wanted to have a friendly conversation with Mr. Ford."

"I'm not accepting visitors at this time," said Fred. "Now step away from my boat."

I racked the slide on the shotgun and raised it to my shoulder. That was enough. They turned and walked away. I kept my weapon trained on them until they disappeared. They didn't look back. I went below to join Fred and Brody.

"I'll be canceling my gambling excursion," Fred said. "I am going to have a talk with whoever runs this place, though."

"You think they were in on it?" asked Brody.

"Probably just took a bribe to let those assholes get close to us," he said.

"How do you deal with that?" I asked.

"I'll pay more to keep them out," he said. "I'll need you two to stay sharp anyway."

"Scope out the approach to the fuel dock," I suggested. "In case we need to toss lines and get out of here."

"I may be accelerating my itinerary," he said. "The sooner I get this deal wrapped up, the sooner we can stop worrying about guys like that."

"I don't think it's wise to hang around here too long," I said. "They may be back better prepared."

"I'll find out what kind of security this place can offer," he said. "I'll be right back."

Brody had stationed herself on the bridge. She was using binoculars to pan the marina.

"I don't like it," she said. "Too many avenues of approach. We're too easy to board at the stern. All three of us can't stay awake forever."

"Let's set up a simple booby trap on the back door," I said. "Another at the starboard entry."

"I'll see what I can find," she said.

I took the binoculars from her and took a look around. I focused on Fred. He was giving the dock master a raft of shit. Then I saw him hand the guy some cash. There were alleys on either side of the marina office, and larger aisles between the condo buildings. Larger yachts blocked my view of portions of the grounds. Brody was right. If we stayed here we were asking for another confrontation. If they came in the middle of the night, whoever was on watch would be outgunned and vulnerable. If they brought reinforcements, we couldn't hold them all off. We were in a poor place strategically. If what they were after was worth as much as Fred claimed, why not show up with twenty heavily-armed men and take it?

I expressed my concerns to Fred when he returned. Brody helped me try to convince him that we should leave immediately. His problem was that he might have to fly out the next day.

He wouldn't know for sure until morning. If we left, we couldn't make it to the next island with an airport until too late in the day. Staniel Cay only had one flight per day back to Florida. From Nassau, he could fly to almost anywhere in the world. We were stuck for at least one night, maybe longer.

Brody asked permission to use a computer for a few minutes. She quickly found what she was looking for. There were three security service companies in Nassau. Each provided uniformed guards. She made a call. She negotiated to have as many men show up as possible, before nightfall.

"They might be able to round up as many as ten men," she said. "They won't be armed."

"We can arm them when they get here," I said. "I feel better already."

"Me too," said Fred. "You two make a hell of a team. I look smarter every day for bringing you with me."

"How far along are you on this business proposition?" I asked.

"Any day now," he said. "Just wrapping up a few odds and ends."

"Get to work," I said. "We'll take care of deploying the guards."

Over the course of two hours, eight men straggled in to report for duty. They came in all shapes and sizes. Some wore ill-fitting uniforms that looked like they'd just come out of storage. Brody lined them up on the dock in front of our boat.

"I've got weapons for those that are willing to carry them," she said.

"Seems like a lot of trouble to stop some petty thieves," said one of the men.

He was sharply dressed and stood with a firm posture. He looked like he had it more together than the rest of the guards.

"What's your name?" Brody asked him.

"Quincy," he replied. "Quincy Perkins."

"Do you know all these guys?"

"Four of us work for the company," he said. "The others are family and friends. We signed them up to make a little extra money tonight."

"We are paying all of you to protect this boat from any and all intruders," she said. "Can you help me keep these men alert to trouble?"

"Yes ma'am," he said. "We won't let nothing happen to your boat."

"Good. I'm going to distribute some guns," she said. "There is very little chance that they'll be necessary. We want to display a show of force. The more menacing we look, the less chance anyone will attempt anything. Understood?"

"Yes, ma'am."

"To be clear," she continued. "No one is to get anywhere near this vessel for any reason."

"I've got it," he said. "We protect your boat. No one gets near it."

Each and every man accepted a weapon. They all stood a little taller once they were armed. They gave the impression that they would honor their duty that night. Fred was down below, working the phones and sending emails. We apprised him of the situation.

"Excellent," he said. "I will be flying out of here tomorrow. You can take the boat away from here as soon as you wish."

"Good news," I said. "How fast do you want us in George Town?"

"I'll be gone at least a week," he said. "Take your time. Make a few stops along the way. Enjoy yourselves."

"What happens if those goons find us after you're gone?" Brody asked.

"I'll have already transferred everything associated with the project," he said. "There will be nothing left for them to steal. We just need to make it one more night."

"They might not believe that," I said.

"Then give them what they want," he said. "Let them take the damn things."

We had eight security guards, four of them misfits. We had the three of us. Eleven guns were locked and loaded. I'm not sure how many laws we were breaking, but we didn't care. Fred's enterprise rested on our ability to protect him for one night. It would all be over the next day. I tried to relax but it was impossible. The reliability of our hired hands was unknown. Brody alternated her time from the bridge, to the deck, and to the dock. She spoke with each man, sizing him up, keeping him alert.

Fred stayed on the phone late into the evening. We could hear computer keys clacking away in the otherwise quiet night. I was restless and nervous. We'd done everything we could to secure *Incognito*, but I wasn't comfortable. I had a disturbing feeling in my gut. Something wasn't right. We weren't sufficiently prepared. I went to find Brody.

"It's not good enough," I told her. "If they want us, they'll come get us."

"We've done an amazing job so far," she said. "We couldn't ask for more."

"These guys will fold when the shit hits the fan," I said. "Or take quick bullets. We are risking their lives as well as our own."

"What do you want to do?" she asked.

"I say we get out of here right now," I said.

"Fred won't go for it," she said. "He's got a flight to catch."

"Then we need to get him out of here," I suggested.

"How? And to where?"

"Let me go talk to him," I said.

Eighteen

I found Fred working furiously. He was transferring large streams of data onto thumb drives. He urged the machine to move faster.

"I've got a bad feeling about this, Fred," I said. "I really think we ought to leave right now."

"I can't stop now," he said. "I'll be finished soon."

"It won't do you any good if you're dead," I told him. "You'll have to postpone your meeting."

"I will not," he said. "I've put my life's blood into this. I've got to catch that plane tomorrow and seal the deal."

"How much longer?"

"An hour maybe."

I had to think of a solution. With each passing minute, I felt more and more like a sitting duck. Brody came to check on us.

"What's the plan?" she asked.

"I'm working on it," I said. "How are our guards doing? Have you got a feel for who we can trust?"

"The four real guards should be okay," she said. "They've seen a few scuffles. The rest of them are next to worthless. Why?"

"The four good ones are going to sneak Fred out of here and get him to the airport," I said. "We'll keep the others aboard as we leave the marina."

"How will they get back home?"

"We'll drop them off on the other side of the island," I said. "Give them some cash for a cab."

"Come talk to Quincy," she said.

She led me to the leader of the crew. He was a good six inches taller than I and more muscular. His skin was black and his teeth were very white. He listened to my instructions intently.

"Take your best three guys," I began. "Sneak Fred out of the marina and get him to the airport. Stay in populated well-lit places once you get there. The four of you keep him surrounded and safe. You are to stay with him until he gets on that plane."

"We can do that," he said. "But what about the boat?"

"We're leaving," I said. "Tonight. Very soon."

"My other men?"

"Do you know the boat ramp over in West Bay?" I asked.

"Yes, it's a big party beach there," he answered.

"I can get them to shore," I assured him. "They can find their way home."

"Shouldn't be a problem," he said. "Let me know when you are ready."

I went back to Fred. Brody stayed on the lookout. Fred was wrapping things up, stowing thumb drives and CDs into a hard case.

"This bird is ready to fly," he said. "By this time tomorrow, next day at the latest, it all comes to an end."

"Four guards are waiting for you," I said. "I'm going to start the engines and prepare to leave."

"I'll be okay," he said. "I haven't been this excited in a long time. Thanks for helping make an old man feel young again."

"Thanks for the boat ride," I said. "Next time let's do it without all the drama."

"Sounds like a plan, Breeze my man."

I escorted Captain Fred to the back deck to meet up with Quincy and his men. Quincy had some ideas of his own.

"It's a short walk to the casino," he said. "No flights are allowed at night in the Bahamas. The Casino runs a shuttle to the airport on demand. He'll be safe there until his flight is ready tomorrow."

"Good idea," I said. "Make it happen."

"I sent a man around the perimeter," he said. "It's clear at the moment. We should go now."

"Do it," I said. "Good luck, Fred."

Fred gave me an imaginary tip of his cap and climbed off the boat. He walked up the dark space between the condo buildings, surrounded by four armed men. He'd be at the casino in minutes. His work here was done, but that would be a hard sell for anyone trying to board us. They'd already tried the subtle approach. If they were coming, they'd bring violent intent.

I instructed the rest of the guards to get on board and take defensive positions. Brody worked to free the lines. I climbed up on the bridge and took one last look around. That's when I saw them. At least a dozen men emerged from the alleys on either side of the marina office. They made no attempt to conceal their weapons.

"Brody, now," I yelled. "We've gotta go."

"One more line," she yelled back.

"Don't miss the boat," I called. "It's leaving the station."

I couldn't see her from where I stood. If she answered me, the sound of gunfire drowned her out. I hesitated to put the boat in gear. Our rag-tag defense started firing back, hopefully giving Brody the cover she needed. A small black face appeared on the ladder.

"She's on," he said. "Go."

I shifted both engines into forward and shoved the throttles up. I heard glass shattering behind me. I almost felt the bullets ripping into the fiberglass of Captain Fred's boat. I accelerated even more. The wake I created sent mega-yachts bobbing and rolling all across the marina. I heard curse words shouted at me. Fred probably wouldn't be welcomed back anytime soon. I crouched down behind the helm in search of protection from stray bullets. My men stopped firing. I peeked back and saw one lone figure popping off rounds from the back deck. Brody had positioned herself behind good cover. She was taking careful aim and squeezing off shots at targets that were well beyond the range of her weapon.

Not only was she smart and pretty, she was cool under pressure. I eased back a bit on the throttles and did a quick visual sweep of the deck below. The men had all taken cover wherever they could find it. None appeared wounded. Bullets had ripped holes in windows and fiberglass all along the starboard side. I imagined the back deck was in even worse condition. I hoped that the rewards Fred was about to reap would lessen any anger he might have about all the damage. We got him out alive. We'd gotten ourselves out alive.

The men on the docks disappeared into the darkness. They had no way of knowing that Fred wasn't on the boat. I had no clue what they might do next, if anything. As far as they knew, the object of their interest was driving out to sea.

"Vessel headed west in Nassau Harbor," came the call on the radio. "Identify yourself."

"It's *Incognito* Harbor Control," I answered. "We suddenly developed the urge to travel. Sorry, I forgot to hail."

"What is your destination?" the voice asked.

"Away from Nassau," I responded. "Have a good night."

I turned the radio off and the radar on. Once I cleared the buoys, I sped up to twenty knots. I could almost hear the fuel evaporating. Brody came up to join me.

"How'd you know I was onboard?" she asked.

"One of your buddies told me," I said. "None too soon."

"One brave one in the bunch," she said. "They all fired until empty. No one bothered to reload. They ran and hid."

"Except you," I said. "Badass Brody. Think you hit any of them?"

"I'm certain I did early in the exchange," she said. "I might have even got one from long distance. Hard to be certain."

"They'll be seeking medical attention," I said. "We drop these guys off and disappear."

"Can we go any faster?"

"I never got a chance to get fuel," I said. "I'm not sure how far we can make it at top speed."

"Work on that," she said. "I'll get ready to run these guys to the beach."

We made a wide arc around the west side of New Providence Island. Only the lights necessary for legal navigation were lit. In the dark, we were unidentifiable. I dimmed the lights on the GPS and found the channel into West Bay. I didn't drop the anchor. Instead, I hovered well offshore as Brody lowered the tender. Four stand-in security guards climbed in behind her. I watched them head for shore. Ten minutes later I heard her before I saw her. I left the helm and helped her raise the tender. There were no signs of activity on the beach or at the boat ramp. We were alone. I spun *Incognito* around and headed back out to sea.

I looked at the fuel flow gauge, figured in tank capacity, guessed at what we'd used already, and decided we had plenty of fuel to make it to Staniel Cay. If I were wrong, we could fuel up at Highbourne Cay, assuming I could maneuver the big boat well enough to get to their fuel dock.

"You know," said Brody. "One minute we're sitting on the beach at Cayo Costa, or at the marina pool. Everything is peaceful and quiet. The next minute we're dodging bullets in Nassau."

"Shit happens," I said.

"No, shit happens to you," she said. "Something about you attracts chaos."

"I didn't ask for this," I argued. "Captain Fred helped us, so we helped him in return."

"At the same time, he was helping us by taking us out of the reach of a hitman."

"That part's on you, missy," I said. "We're in this together."

"I guess you're right," she admitted. "But is it always going to be this way?"

"An excellent question," I said. "I seem to enjoy long periods of relative calm, punctuated by episodes of pandemonium."

"Which I get to endure along with you."

"Endeavor to persevere," I said. "That's what a smart woman once told me."

"So what's next?" she asked.

"Work our way down to George Town," I said. "Hand Fred his bullet-riddled boat back. Go home."

"Outsmart an assassin, take possession of our boat, and then what?"

"I haven't thought that far ahead," I said. "I've been a bit busy."

"Can you at least consider the possibility of getting another boat over here?" she asked. "Not going back?"

"I have to get *Miss Leap*," I said. "You won't change my mind about that."

"I didn't figure I would," she said. "Just throwing it out for discussion."

We were entering the Exuma Banks as the sun came up. The water was clear and blue. Orange streaks came down from the sunrise to mix an exotic cocktail of colors on the horizon. The low islands of the upper Exumas came into view. I was tired. The adrenaline rush of the previous night had long since ended. Brody was yawning every minute or two. I gave up on the idea of making it to Staniel and diverted for Highbourne. We anchored amidst a dozen other yachts, all much larger than ours. Sleep came quickly.

That sleep was interrupted by a ringing sound. It stopped before I could find the source. It was coming from somewhere in the main salon. Just as I turned to go back to bed, it started again. I dug through drawers and tossed pillows until I found a ringing phone. The caller ID said Me.

"Hello?"

"It's me, Breeze," said Captain Fred. "I'm on the plane. Thought you'd want to know."

"That's fantastic news," I said.

"How'd you fare?" he asked. "How's the boat?"

"We're alive," I said. "The boat is going to need a lot of patching up."

"Patching up? Why?"

"A few hundred bullet holes," I said. "All the back glass is blown out."

"Jesus Christ, Breeze," he said. "What the hell happened?"

"They came for you right after you left," I said. "We barely slipped out in time."

"You were right," he said. "I can't imagine what would have happened if I hadn't listened to you."

"The important thing is that we are all okay," I said. "The boat can be fixed."

"The important thing is that I'm about to pass go and collect a few billion dollars," he said. "I'll buy a new damn boat. Hell, I'll buy you one too."

"You can talk to Brody about that," I said. "I've already got a boat, though."

"I'll be down there in a week," he said. "Gotta go. About to take off."

I put the phone where I could find it easier next time. Brody was still asleep, so I rejoined her.

We didn't wake up until mid-afternoon. We were dirty and hungry. I lost the coin toss, so she got a shower while I fixed breakfast. I noticed we were low on bacon. I cleaned up after we ate and decided to take the tender into the marina to look around. Getting *Incognito* to the fuel dock would be difficult. I tied up at a floating dock and was immediately greeted by security.

"State your business," he said.

"You got any bacon?" I asked.

He chuckled and led me to a tiny store next to the marina office. I was instructed that we were allowed to visit the store and the restaurant, but not the rest of the island. The restaurant happened to be closed that day. I spent ten bucks on a pound of bacon.

We spent a few hours on the beach, even though we weren't supposed to be there. No one came to run us off. Other folks were ferried back and forth from the mega-yachts. We pretended we belonged. Having rich folks look down their nose at me was nothing compared to being shot at. Besides, Brody was the hottest girl on the beach.

We enjoyed the sunset and a good meal. We tried to relax. We had jumped out of the frying pan and into a tropical paradise. There was no reason to think we were in any danger there. Soon, Fred's project would be made public, and the bad guys would leave us alone. The danger would be back in Florida. It was up to me to figure out what to do about that. I didn't yet have a clue. I did have a thirst for rum. Brody joined me for several shots of the expensive stuff out of Fred's liquor cabinet. It eased any remaining tension like a magic elixir.

We left for Staniel the next day. I called the fuel dock before approaching. They asked that we anchor and wait for slack tide to come in. The cross-current near the dock was troublesome for larger vessels. We did as instructed. It gave us a chance to visit the swimming pigs on Big Majors Cay. The dangers we had faced seemed a million miles away. Brody laughed and squealed when approached by the pigs.

We got our fuel and continued south to Little Farmers Cay. It was a route I had taken before. I'd traveled with Holly and her hippie crew a few years back. I wondered what she was up to. The last time I'd spoken to her she said she was looking for crew for another Bahamas trip. I started looking for her boat. It would not surprise me if *Another Adventure* suddenly appeared. It had happened before.

The following day we made it down to Elizabeth Harbour. We anchored across the bay from George Town at Sand Dollar Beach. We had a few days to kill before Fred arrived. We spent them sitting in the water drinking beer, and making love. It was a proper reward after what we'd been through. We picked up groceries at the Exuma Market after walking through town. The hurricanes had mostly spared the island, but old Redboone's Café had burnt to the ground. Cruisers and cab drivers had found another place to congregate.

Fred finally called to announce his impending arrival. We moved his boat to the Redshanks anchorage and spent a day putting duct tape over bullet holes. I found a tarp to hang over the rear glass that was no longer there. We cleaned up any remaining fragments that we could find and generally made the boat presentable. She'd been good to us, even though we'd put her through hell. I patted the transom and thanked her for her service.

"Sorry, girl," I said. "I'm sure Fred will get you back shipshape in no time."

When he got out of the cab from the airport, he looked like a man who'd just made a few billion bucks. His smile never ended. He hugged us both. He tipped the cabbie a hundred dollar bill.

"Have you seen the news?" he asked. "I've been all over the TV."

"Sorry, no we haven't," I said. "It's a pretty big deal I take it."

"Big doesn't describe it, boy," he said. "Microsoft and Apple had to merge resources to get it. It's all theirs now. All I have to do is figure out what to do with all my money."

"Congratulations," said Brody. "That's amazing."

"I owe the two of you," he said. "You can name your price. Whatever you want."

Brody and I looked at each other. What are you supposed to say to that? A true friend of mine was now worth billions. He was offering me a piece of it. I suppose I had earned it, but I wasn't comfortable setting a price on our friendship.

"I really don't know what to say," I told him. "We would have helped you for nothing."

"I know that," he said. "You don't have to go overboard. How's a million bucks sound?"

"That's ridiculous," I said.

"Really, Fred," said Brody. "It's too much. We can't accept that."

"I'll give half to you and half to the charity of your choice," he offered. "And I'll buy you a new boat when you make up your mind about it."

I didn't need the money. Brody and I were already sitting on a pile, but I couldn't let some charity miss out on half a million bucks. It only took two seconds to decide which one.

"Enduring Warrior," I said. "We'll take the money provided they get half."

"Consider it done," he said. "I'll show you the receipt when I get it."

"We trust you," I said. "Our half needs to be in cash."

"Not a problem," he said. "Let's shake on it."

Enduring Warrior got their money. I would have preferred it to be anonymous, but Fred donated it in my name. He laughed at all the holes in his boat. He laughed when it rained. He laughed loudly and freely at just about anything that happened. Funny how a few billion dollars can lighten one's mood. He had the world by the ass and he was enjoying it.

Brody and Fred worked out the details on a cash transfer to an account in the States that we could access. We wouldn't be able to carry that much cash on the plane. I didn't even know where we'd put it on the boat once we got it. Brody suggested that we leave it in the bank. It sounded like a foreign thought at first, but obviously, it made perfect sense. I thought I might even get me one of them smartphones.

Nineteen

Fred paid for our flight back to Florida. After landing in Fort Myers, we got a hotel room close to the airport. I needed some time to consider the man who might be hunting us. Was he still on the job? We'd been mostly gone for months. Our boat had been unoccupied for a long time. Surely he'd given up looking for us. I wanted to call Diver Dan, but we didn't have his number. I knew that he left his business cards in various places around Fort Myers Beach. It would be easy enough to locate one, but that would put us in the center of our assassin's search area.

I decided that there was no way he was still sitting in town, waiting for us to return. It was more likely that he'd paid someone to notify him the minute they saw us return. If that were the case, we'd have time to get to the boat and leave town before he could get to us. He'd discover that the boat was gone soon enough. What else would he have to go on? Did someone at the FBI hand him a file that contained our likely whereabouts and favored haunts?

We could not return to the marina. He'd have someone there to alert him of our return. We'd have to figure out what to do about the car we'd left there. The other obvious places for him to search were Punta Gorda and Pelican Bay. I thought he'd have a hard time getting to us in Pelican Bay. He could only approach by boat. It would be hard to hide a weapon wearing shorts and a T-shirt. I suppose he could keep it in a bag or a cooler.

If we simply avoided any of the places that we were known to frequent, he couldn't possibly track us down. On the other hand, we'd be looking over our shoulder for the rest of our lives. Could we draw him out and take him down without getting ourselves killed? I consulted with Brody on that possibility.

"There are so many factors to consider," she said. "The lay of the land or buildings. Will we have any advance notice of his presence? Does one of us act as a decoy?"

"We have to assume that if he was contracted by the FBI, he's damn good," I said. "In my mind I see him popping out of nowhere and pulling the trigger before we even know he's there."

"How do we defend against that?" she asked.

"I don't know," I admitted. "We can't allow that to happen. We have to arrange for it to happen at a time and place of our choosing somehow. On familiar turf. Someplace we can spot him before he can shoot."

"How will we know him when we see him?"

"We have to hope he stands out somehow," I said. "That he looks out of place in the environment."

"Hope is not a strategy," she said.

"We can make a stand or we can run," I said. "If we stand it will be over soon enough. We may die or we may kill him first. If we run, we run forever. Change our names and move to Idaho like you said."

"I wasn't serious about that," she said. "What if we stand and no one shows up?"

"We can assume it's over," I said. "But we'll never know for sure."

"I don't know, Breeze," she said. "It's a lot to think about."

"First we get *Miss Leap* back," I said. "That's why we're here."

"What's your gut telling you?" she asked.

"That we'll drive away from Fort Myers Beach," I said. "And that we'll be confronted sometime after that, if we stick around southwest Florida."

"Or we may never see it coming," she said. "We'll just take a bullet and be gone."

"Possible, but not likely," I said. "We're already hyper-vigilant. Our combined skills should alert us in time. They'll have to."

"I suspect he'll have equal or greater skills," she said. "That's what worries me."

Brody had another handgun on the boat. I had my shotgun, but I couldn't carry it around in public. I could see no other course of action but to get on the boat and depart Fort Myers Beach immediately. Brody reluctantly agreed. We'd arm up and keep our eyes and ears open. We had the airport shuttle drop us off at the Matanzas Inn.

I found Diver Dan's business card in the laundry room across the street from the office. He answered on the second ring.

"Where are you?" he asked.

"Laundry room," I said. "Tell me what you've seen out there. Anyone poking around our boat?"

"Not for a long time," he said. "Right after you left the last time, a guy was out there on the water taxi circling around. He visited a few of your neighbors too."

As I had suspected, one or more of those neighbors had been enlisted in the hitman's cause. He probably made up some story about trying to get in touch with me. They'd call him as soon as they saw us get on the boat.

"Can you pick us up at the dinghy dock after dark?" I asked.

"Ten o'clock okay?"

"Make it eleven," I said. "And thanks."

"What have you gotten into this time?" he asked.

"Long story," I said. "Don't know when I can tell you about it. We'll be leaving tonight."

"Do I need to be armed when I come to get you?"

"Your choice," I said. "Probably not, but it wouldn't hurt."

"You make me question our friendship sometimes, Breeze," he said.

"We can find another ride," I said. "If it's too much trouble."

"No," he said. "Once upon a time you made me wealthy. I haven't forgotten."

"See you at eleven then?"

"I'll be there."

We needed to kill some time. The gunman wouldn't know we were in town yet. We walked the few blocks to Times Square and ordered a pizza. We walked on the beach amongst the thousands of tourists at sunset. We blended in with the crowd as best we could. Both of us carefully observed every person we encountered. We saw no gun bulges under Hawaiian shirts. I didn't smell danger in the air. As usual, Brody had her weapon in her purse. I noticed that her hand never strayed far from it.

"You okay?" I asked.

"Just feeling a little anxious," she said. "We're so exposed."

"Darkness won't help your anxiety any," I said. "You want to walk down the well-lit street or take the back alleys?"

"Alleys," she said. "You ready?"

We snuck from building to building like we knew our adversary was on the street looking for us, even though I was sure he wasn't. We walked under the bridge, hopping from piling to piling, searching the darkness in front of us for anything suspicious. We hid behind the porta-potty adjacent to the dinghy dock. It stunk. Diver Dan showed up right on time. He didn't have to tie up to the dock. We jumped in, he hit reverse, and we made our way out into the harbor.

My first glimpse of *Leap of Faith* gave me hope. She had always been my refuge. I felt that if I could fire up her engine and take off, everything would be okay.

"She's been sitting a while," said. Dan. "You want me to stick around to make sure she starts?"

"Good idea," I said. "But she'll start. I've got faith in her."

"What do we do if it doesn't start?" asked Brody. "Stick around Dan."

"She'll start," was all I said.

It was my hope that the neighbors were asleep and no one had made a phone call yet. The engine noise could possibly wake them, so we had no time to dick around. I entered through the aft cabin door and went straight to the lower helm. I turned the key on, advanced the throttle slightly, and pushed the start button. The old Lehman engine sparked to life on the first crank. I took it as a good sign. She smoked a little, but that would go away once she warmed up. I waved off Diver Dan. He nodded and wished us well.

Brody went to the bow to untie the mooring pennant. I went up on the bridge. As soon as we were free of the mooring ball I steered us through the field of boats and under the Matanzas Bridge. We went out the Pass and into the Gulf under a starry sky.

Brody brought the handguns up.

"The second one has a little surface rust," she said. "But the action still works."

"Once we get far enough offshore you can test fire it," I said. "I'd like to take a couple shots with it too."

"Let me clean it up and oil it first," she said. "Your shotgun too."

"That's my girl," I said. "Go do your thing. I'm good up here for now."

As the night wore on, I started having doubts. I tried to think like a hired killer. If I needed someone dead, I figured there wasn't much they could do about it once I found them. They'd never see me coming, never know what hit them. I searched for something positive about our chosen strategy. A boat was easy to defend as long as it was anchored. I could see another boat approaching from a long way off. Anyone who got too close would be an easy target. The problem was, we'd have to step foot off the boat sooner or later. We'd need food. We'd need booze. We couldn't last forever. Land would be dangerous unless we went someplace totally unfamiliar to us. The nearest place to get groceries that I'd never been was the Tampa/Saint Pete area. It was a long haul from Pelican Bay.

What were we supposed to do once we anchored in Pelican Bay? Would we just sit on the boat waiting for someone to attempt to kill us? Should we hope they showed up soon and failed? I figured it would drive us crazy sooner than later, but I could think of no other options. If we wanted this to end, this was the way to do it. Draw him in, and take him out.

Brody brought the weapons up to the bridge.

"Locked and loaded," she said. "What do you say we toss a water bottle over and see who hits it first?"

"Ready when you are," I said.

She tossed the bottle over the side. We let it drift behind us about fifteen feet.

"Now," she said.

I squeezed off a round and missed by a foot. Her first shot came within an inch of the target. I fired again and missed by two feet. Her second shot was a direct hit.

"If the shit hits the fan, you're going to have to do a lot better than that," she said.

I traded weapons with her. My first attempt with her gun was a close miss, maybe two inches. She fired my gun and missed by a foot. All the misses had been low and to the left. I tried her gun again and nicked the bottle.

"Not too bad," she said. "I think the sights are off on this thing."

"Are they adjustable?" I asked.

"It's going to take a lot of tinkering to get them right," she said. "A rocking boat isn't exactly the best shooting platform."

"Let me try it again," I said.

I aimed high and to the right. The bottle was now twenty feet away. I almost hit it. If I were shooting at a man's heart, I'd have hit him in the gut.

"That's damn good at that distance," she said. "Let me get another bottle."

We tried again at fifteen feet but with a faster aim.

"Raise and shoot," she said. "The bad guy is raising his weapon too."

After some practice, I was able to put my bullets within a foot diameter circle all around the bottle. I never did hit it when trying to shoot quickly, but my shots would be within the torso of a human target. Brody hit the bottle with a third of her attempts.

I felt no shame in losing our little contest. I was proud of her. She was obviously the one who should take the shot at our potential attacker, but we'd have no control over how it went down.

We entered the Boca Grande Pass as the sun rose over Charlotte Harbor. A half-dozen boats were well-spaced in Pelican Bay. I took us to the southern end, as far from the other boats as possible. I anchored just off a very shallow grass flat. No boats had any reason to attempt to traverse the flat. They'd run aground. Anyone trying it would be a suspect. I let Brody get some sleep while I maintained watch. I saw nothing more interesting than mullet fishermen throwing a cast net. After I got a nap, we discussed potential outcomes.

"As long as one of us is awake," I said. "No one will be able to approach our boat without a deadly response."

"I think we're fine as long as we're sitting here at anchor," she said. "But if we sit here too long doing nothing, life won't be much worth living."

"You're right," I said. "We've lost our freedom over this. Let's hope he tries something soon."

A week went by and no boogeyman appeared. We'd run out of good food and had resorted to eating out of cans. Between the cash I had stashed on the boat and the money from Fred in the bank, we had a million dollars, but we had canned chili for dinner. Not being able to fish for dinner was the cost of vigilance. I tried fishing off the boat, but could only hook under-sized trout and catfish. I could have tried harder, but I didn't want to be distracted from my constant surveillance of everything around me.

Brody was bored out of her mind, but she did her best to match my awareness level.

"Come on, you bastard," she said. "We're just sitting here waiting for you. Let's get this over with."

"Do you want to pull up and run for supplies?" I asked. "We can be in Saint Pete in two days if we push it."

"Then we start this cycle all over again," she said. "Let's give it a few more days. You would think he'd have a ranger or volunteer tell him that we're here."

"Maybe he can't get a boat," I said. "Maybe he's afraid of boats. He just can't get to us."

"Coming on the ferry wouldn't help him," she said. "Unless he rented a kayak to paddle out to us."

"He'd be way too vulnerable on a kayak," I said. "I wouldn't try it."

"What about at night?" she asked. "We wouldn't hear him."

"I suppose he could rent a campsite," I said. "Walk across the island in the dark. Paddle out here and try to whack us both."

"Yea, doesn't sound likely," she said. "So where is he? Why hasn't he shown up?"

"Maybe it's over," I said. "Maybe he gave up the hunt. Maybe the FBI reined him in."

Another week went by. We were beginning to think that all our preparations and diligence were a waste of time. We were almost disappointed that our hitman had failed to show. We were coming to the conclusion that he would never show up. We'd made ourselves extremely visible in the place that I visited most. I called Pelican Bay home. If he couldn't find us there he was a poor excuse for an assassin. Our freezer was empty. Our pantry was empty. We needed water.

I used the bat phone to call Fed-Ex Fred. I asked him to see what he could learn from the FBI. He called back the next day. The alleged hitman had fallen off the face of the Earth. There'd been no contact, despite efforts to reach him. It had been over three months since we'd first learned of his existence. Now we wondered if he ever existed at all. I thought maybe the story had been concocted just to fuck with Brody. The idea that someone within the FBI would hire a hitman while the Bureau swirled in controversy grew more and more preposterous.

"I think this is all a bunch of bullshit," I told Brody.

"I'm starting to think the same," she said. "Something would have happened by now."

"Screw it," I said. "Let's go to town. Get a hot shower. Get some decent food."

"Amen to that," she said.

"Fort Myers Beach or the marina?" I asked.

"We've got a car at the marina," she said. "We need to do something about that anyway."

"The marina it is."

I called the marina on the radio as we approached. I was advised that they'd kept our slip available, but we owed them three month's rent. I assured them that wouldn't be a problem. I was relieved to get our old spot back. Having the car would make the grocery shopping an easy task. We quickly reunited with the old gang. There was one new face in the crowd. The dark-haired man with abnormally white skin was living aboard a near-derelict fishing boat. He introduced himself as Mark. He was obviously not a Floridian, or at least he had an aversion to the sun. He didn't fit in with the rest of the group. He was friendly enough though. He drank beer and swapped tales just like the rest of them. I filed my observations away for future discussion with Brody.

We filled our pantry and freezer. We enjoyed hot showers. I settled the bill with the marina. Captain Fred called to tell us about the hundred-foot Hatteras he was having custom built. He wanted to know if I'd be interested in delivering it to him in the Bahamas when it was finished. I told him I'd be happy to. We fell right back into the marina life like we'd never left. Brody was happy there. When I suggested that Derelict Mark was suspicious, she dismissed it as paranoia. She put her fears behind her. I urged her to remain vigilant, just in case. We still carried our weapons at all times.

It happened late one night in the spring. We were on our way to the hot tub. I had my gun under a towel. Brody had hers in a beach bag. No one else was about, except Derelict Mark. He was standing with his back to us, in front of a barbecue grill. It was the grill intended for the use of the condo residents. The boaters had their own grill. That was my first clue. The second was that I could see that the grill was not lit. There was no smoke or smell of cooking food. All of my senses went on full alert.

I jabbed Brody with an elbow while cocking my chin towards the man at the grill. He turned slowly to face us. Time froze for me. The light above his head glinted off the cold steel in his hand. His silenced pistol started to rise. His face wore a disturbing grin. I stepped in front of Brody while raising my own weapon. He was fifteen feet away. Somehow I remembered to aim high and to the right. I was just squeezing the trigger when I heard the shot. I followed through with a shot of my own. The hitman never got a chance to fire. BAP BAP. Two rounds hit him square in the chest. Mine was just slightly low and left of center. Brody's was two inches to the right of mine. I don't know how she got her weapon up and shot before me, but I'd witnessed it. I'd been instantly decisive. I recognized the threat and moved as fast as I could to neutralize it. She'd been a split second quicker. Together we had eliminated him.

I kicked his gun to the side and crouched down to inspect the damage. Brody covered me, weapon still poised to shoot. His eyes stared off into nowhere. The last breath escaped his lungs. "Is it over?" she asked.

"It is," I said. "It's finally over."

"Amen to that," she said.

There would be many questions to answer, so in that sense, it wasn't fully over. The threat, however, was gone. There would be police and lawyers and maybe even judges, but we had the two Freds on our side. We also had some leverage with the FBI. If they didn't want the world to know what they'd done to us, it would be brushed under the rug.

It would all work out. Shit always works out.

Author's Thoughts

I want to thank Troy Warshel for introducing me to **Operation Enduring Warrior**, and for his service to our country. For more information or to donate please visit http://enduringwarrior.org/

As of early January 2018, *Leap of Faith* has fully recovered from the impact of Hurricane Irma. We were more fortunate than those who lost their vessels to the storm. Many of our friends and acquaintances in the Keys suffered greatly.

For those who will be disappointed that I interjected politics into this story; Brody was an FBI agent. The FBI is in the news on a daily basis. It couldn't be ignored. Consider it as an example of how politics intrudes into our everyday lives, even for someone as apolitical as Breeze.

As always, if you wish to have your name become a character in Breeze's adventures, or wish to share ideas for future plotlines, feel free to contact me at Kimandedrobinson@gmail.com

Yes, we looked at a boat in South Carolina. No, we didn't buy it.

I got an email from Captain Fred that inspired me to bring back his character. *Incognito* suffered no actual bullet wounds during the creation of this story. I've never met Fed-Ex Fred.

Acknowledgements

Proofreading Team: Dave Calhoun, Jeanene Olson, Laura Spink

Final Edit: John Corbin

Cover design by https://ebooklaunch.com/

Interior formatting by https://ebooklaunch.com/

Other Books in the Series

Trawler Trash; Confessions of a Boat Bum
http://amzn.to/2E37afw

Following Breeze http://amzn.to/2fXJgq2

Free Breeze http://amzn.to/2fXILfv

Redeeming Breeze http://amzn.to/2gbBjAx

Bahama Breeze http://amzn.to/2fJiMe6

Cool Breeze http://amzn.to/2weKg11

True Breeze http://amzn.to/2ws6Hzp

Ominous Breeze http://amzn.to/2lPzg70

Restless Breeze http://amzn.to/2Aicj0A

Other Books by Ed Robinson

Leap of Faith; Quit Your Job and Live on a Boat http://amzn.to/2fFeJwh

Poop, Booze, and Bikinis http://amzn.to/2lOvOZN

The Untold Story of Kim http://amzn.to/2Cy0Cbr

Contact Ed Robinson at Kimandedrobinson@gmail.com

Ed's Blog: https://quityourjobandliveonaboat.com/

Facebook: https://www.facebook.com/quityourjobandliveonaboat/